THE SANFT SASQUATCH

THE SANFT SASQUATCH

A Sammi Cupertino Canadian Paranormal Cozy Mystery

EERIE FALLS MYSTERIES
BOOK II

ALYN TROY

"Oh, Sammi," Lenora Needles said, as she pushed through the door to the bookshop. I made sure it closed behind her. Even though the calendar said spring, April in Southern Ontario was no time to leave a door open. "I haven't had the chance to congratulate you on your romance with our new officer of the law. A pity that you and my son Robert never connected."

The knitting and notions shop owner smiled as she pulled off her gloves, then thrust them in her pocket. Her oversized bag hung from a shoulder. Red yarn impaled by two blue knitting needles peeked out of the bag.

"Boys aren't my thing." I raised an eyebrow. Courtney and I had been dating three months now. And Mrs. Needles really meant she hadn't found an excuse to fish for gossip from me. I wondered what she was after to bring her in today.

"Well, I wish you the best. I'm sure Robert will be happy for you too. We're having dinner tonight. He's coming in from

Toronto this evening. Says a friend of his is playing at the bar tonight."

"Um. Thanks. I'll tell Courtney you stopped by." I kept my tone polite and knew from years of interaction with the town gossip to not say any more than necessary. "Were you looking for anything in particular today that I can help you find?"

"Well, is your grandfather here?"

"Not yet," I said politely. "He rarely arrives this early. He should be along in another hour when he takes over the shop for the afternoon."

That nosy wench is fishing for details on Merlin and Betty! The mental voice of Cleo, my undead cat, filtered into my mind. *Tell her to go pound sand. Preferably in the Sahara.*

Mrs. Needles' eyes darted around the shop, settling on the staircase along the side wall of the store that ascended to Gramps's study above us. "Or is Merlin still spending late nights and early mornings with that widowed witch, Betty Grindlespool?"

I kept my customer service smile plastered on my face but turned to tap the stuffed owl on our checkout counter. The owl's eyes glowed with a red magical light. The sign that there was a mundane in our store. Witch was a term we fae could use as a polite title or as an insult. Mrs. Needles' tone left no doubt which witch she implied.

"How rude!" DeAnn Powers said, stepping out from behind one of our free-standing book stacks near the back of the store. Trust DeAnn, with no knowledge of fae, to get the implied use right off. "Lenora! You should take that back. Betty is a wonderful lady, and it's none of your business if she's keeping company with a man."

"Oh. Hello Miss Powers," Lenora Needles stammered, her cheeks glowing red to match the owl's eyes.

DeAnn crossed her arms over her cable knit maroon sweater and stared at Eerie Falls' number one gossip monger. "You know, I think I figured out what's missing from my newest mystery series. The town gossip. Always sticking her nose where it doesn't belong and stirring up trouble just to feel important."

Mrs. Needles's brow dropped, and she scrunched her eyes tight to glare at the author. "I'd best not see my name in any of your books."

"Oh, I aways change the names to protect the guilty," DeAnn said, her own smile growing. "I wonder if Laverna Bechard would work for a gossip character."

"Wasn't Laverna the Roman goddess of thieves?" I asked, rolling a lip in, very aware of what that name meant.

"And Bechard is a name that means gossip," DeAnn said with a nod. "Of course, it sees common usage now, and there are many good people with the last name. But astute readers will recognize the name for what it is."

Mrs. Needles eyes darted back and forth between DeAnn and I. "Well, I never expected that kind of greeting right here in Eerie Falls."

"Then, perhaps you should aspire to not be the town gossip," DeAnn said, her eyes locked on Mrs. Needles. "I'm sure that Merlin and Betty can have a nice dinner together, without telling you about their social schedule."

"So they are seeing each other." Mrs. Needles' eyes squinted even tighter, her mouth hardening into a fine line. She turned toward me, gave a nod, and jerked the front door open. "Good day, Sammi."

To say Mrs. Needles used a forceful tug to close the door behind her would have been an understatement. Fortunately, the piston mechanism on it kept her from being able to slam it. I heard Cleo's mental chuckle. Her sleek, grey, Abyssinian cat form jumped up onto the counter. I absently reached out to stroke her.

That was so perfect! Cleo's thought came into my mind. *I've wanted to tell that old witch off for decades but polite society and all.*

I raised an eyebrow since I knew my grams had done exactly that several times. She must miss that activity to bring it up again.

"Oh, dear," DeAnn said, dropping onto the tall stool in front of our checkout counter. "I hope I didn't make an enemy there."

"If you're not gossiping with Mrs. Needles," I said with a chuckle, "then she's probably gossiping about you."

"That's how town gossips work, don't they?" DeAnn shrugged and set a couple of books on the counter. I scanned them into our computer, and a total with the Value Added Tax, or VAT, showed on the tablet facing the client side of the counter.

DeAnn tapped her debit card to the pad.

I glanced at the titles as I slid the books towards her and gave a light chuckle.

"Those titles don't move very often. *Respecting the Government of Ontario.* That is one to fight off insomnia."

The author dropped the books into her cloth shopping bag. "Well, if I'm writing about a small town here in the province, then I need to understand the interactions of the various ministers, and is it a premier? Or Lieutenant Governor?"

"Ontario is a parliamentary system," I said, trying to think back to my classes many years before and trying to stick to the mundane systems. DeAnn didn't need to know about how the fae government interacted with our mundane cousins. "The Lieutenant Governor acts like a chief executive on behalf of His Majesty, but the duties are few and mostly ceremonial."

"I assumed they were much like a governor of one of the U.S. states?" DeAnn nodded. "Then what is the premier?"

"The premier might actually be closer to the governor of your state of New York," I said as the front door opened. My smile brightened when I spied Courtney, wearing her uniform jacket and knitted Provincial Police toque. That was one of the few things Mrs. Needles insisted on, providing cold weather hats and mittens made by her local knitting club for our two town constables.

"Nice hat," I said with a chuckle. "Mrs. Needles was just in here."

"She didn't look too happy when she stomped by me," Courtney said, and leaned over the counter. I got a quick kiss from her before she grabbed the open tall stool I kept there.

"Well, I only told her I was going to put her in one of my books," DeAnn said with a strong sarcastic tone. "I've no idea why she wouldn't want to be known as the town's gossip monger."

"That'll do it." Courtney chuckled. "Did I interrupt your nefarious plotting? Will Mrs. Needles be the perp or the suspect in the latest mystery?"

"Hmmmm.... That probably depends on whether the real Mrs. Needles behaves herself." DeAnn chuckled and gave us a sly look. "I've got a coffee mug back in New York that says *I'm an author. Honk me off, and I'll kill you in my next book.*"

"Be careful with that," Courtney said with a grin. "If Mrs. Needles turned up dead, that mug could be considered an indication of motive."

"Oh. I would never harm someone in real life. But fiction-ally, I do that all the time." DeAnn's eyes twinkled, and her mouth curled up with mirth, as she glanced out to the street. "Oh!"

Outside, a panel van, one that easily could have carried a logo for a plumber or other home service contractor, pulled up on our side of the street. But that wasn't what caught DeAnn's attention.

"I know it's still nippy," she said with a nod to the tall figure that emerged from the far side and stood staring across the road at Darcy's bar. "I mean, a full Bigfoot costume? Isn't that overkill for this time of year?"

Courtney and I shared a glance. She rose from the stool. "I'll go ask them to back up and not be so close to the hydrant."

I knew she meant she would warn the real Sasquatch that there was a mundane in town. We really didn't need the author writing Bigfoot into a mystery book, did we?

DeAnn shrugged and turned back to stroke Cleo's chin and cheeks. "I really should see about getting a cat now that I've got a real rental in town."

"Did Mr. McGristle say if you're allowed pets?"

She shrugged. "I think he said nothing over twelve pounds. Surely a cat like Cleo doesn't weight that much."

I should say not, Cleo's voice scoffed in my mind, as she turned away from DeAnn's touch. *I'm barely up to eight pounds. Of course, my diet shifted radically when I grabbed this body.*

I rolled my lower lip in, so I didn't blab out my response to Cleo.

"Oh, I hope I didn't offend the little dear," DeAnn asked, tilting her head to watch Cleo. Fortunately, Cleo stood and leaned into the author's outstretched hand again.

"She's a lady. Best not to inquire about her weight," I volunteered with a chuckle.

I glanced outside. The driver of the van had his door open and watched the curb as he backed the panel van up another foot. Across the street, the Sasquatch, now in human form, stood with a petite Asian girl. Both wore coats. Or, if my suspicion was correct, the Sasquatch wore an illusion to make his own furry form resemble a furry jacket.

Courtney nodded to the driver and then headed back to the bookshop. But she paused and held the door open for our other town cop, Sergeant Lorne Pebblebrook. He waved a woman with jet black hair and steel-grey eyes in first. Everything about the woman screamed high fashion, and not in a good way. She wore an expensive T3 designer coat, one from top fae designer Thaddeus Trevor Thurburg III, or better known as T3. She also sported the latest T3 knee-high slouch boots. Her thin and high heels were barely passable for this time of year. Despite the warming weather, there was still too much ice around for walking far in those.

Courtney's face slid into what I teasingly called her cop face. Emotionless. But her eyes had hardened.

"Excellent, you're both here. Mizz Durand, this is Sammi Cupertino, owner of our town's bookstore," Lorne said, coming in behind the woman. "And this is our *visitor* from New York State, Miss Powers."

Lorne added extra emphasis on both the miss title for the woman and on *visitor* for DeAnn. The way Lorne said *mizz* let me know that Ms. Durand was pushing her social status as a replacement for a real title.

She pulled her leather gloves off and held her hand out toward DeAnn. "I'm Niki Durand, Special Assistant to Giles Neverwind, MPP. Pleased to make your acquaintance, Miss Powers."

"Likewise," DeAnn stayed polite, but even she was being cautious around the newcomer. "What's an MPP?"

"Minister of the Provincial Parliament," Lorne explained. "Minister Neverwind represents the riding that includes Eerie Falls."

Chuckles Neverwind is anything but what his surname implies, Cleo's laugh intruded into my thoughts. *He always eating something he shouldn't. Though I suspect he tried snooping where he shouldn't have and caught a curse that makes him gassy.*

"What does a special assistant to our MPP do?" I inquired, extending my hand. Niki took it, and her eyes lingered on my face for a second before she smiled one of the most political smiles I had ever seen on a political type.

"In this case, I'm researching how our provincial agencies are performing," Durand said. "Police and other agencies."

"Snooping, she means," Courtney said. "Hello Niki. Didn't expect to see you slumming it out here in the... what did you used to call this part of Ontario, you know, the parts that weren't Toronto or Ottawa?"

"You mean the various ridings, Court?" Niki said, her eyes and voice both going cold as she looked at my girlfriend. The air between them picked up an electric sizzle that almost devolved into the beginning of a spell feud.

"Evidently," Lorne interjected, his voice in a friendly tone, "you and our new constable know each other?"

"Roommates our first semester at university," Courtney said, her eyes glued to the newcomer. "At least until she pledged to a sorority and moved out of the residence building."

"You should have pledged with me," Durand said with a sweet yet insincere smile. "I tried to get you to. Pity. You missed out on a great sisterhood. Our cov–" her eyes shifted to DeAnn, "house was made up of all sorts of future leaders."

She'd almost said *coven*, which told me it was the fae sorority on campus. Several of Toronto's top covens used the university's Greek houses as training covens. Since we fae didn't get our full powers until our mid-thirties, our twenties were spent learning a lot about our magical natures.

"Criminology and the... sisterhoods don't mix," Courtney said, then her cheeks flared red, and her eyes shifted to DeAnn. She'd almost added *magical* to the term sisterhood but caught herself.

"That's why you should have gone into Political Science," Durand said, shaking her head. "I tried to warn you that you'd end up in some cheap little podunk backwater like Eerie Falls."

$\frac{1}{2}$ 2 $\frac{1}{2}$

"So..." I said half an hour later when Courtney and I slid into a booth at Eerie Taps. "What's up with you and MIZZ Durand?"

"Umm.... Nothing?" Courtney shrugged and leaned to hang her police coat on the hook attached to the wooden end of the booth. I did the same with my coat. It was late, but there were still a few patrons in the pub for the afternoon. Bubbles, owner of one set of tourist cabins outside of town, sat next to a gent wearing civilian clothes and a Royal Canadian Navy ball cap. From here, I couldn't see which ship it noted.

Darcy, local vampire and tavern owner, stepped up to our booth right then.

"Heard you honked off Mrs. Needles, Sammi."

"Wasn't me!" I raised my hands defensively. "Did she come in here gossiping?"

Darcy chuckled and tipped her head to the bar. "My new

10

girl came in right as our local gossip ran out of your shop. The way she described the perp, it had to be Mrs. Needles."

"New girl?" I glanced over at the bar. A woman with pixie highlights was pulling a pint from one of the taps behind the bar.

"Zoey Breeze. We'd been seeing each other whenever I could get up to Toronto. Convinced her to move down here and help in the bar. I might actually get to sleep in through the afternoons once she's fully trained."

"Breeze?" Courtney pursed her lips. "I knew a Joey Breeze at university. Real flighty. Even for a pixie. I wonder if he's related to your girlfriend?"

Darcy's smile grew ever so slightly. "I'll send her over with your drinks. What will it be today?"

"Burger, Diet Coke," I said, since Courtney was still staring at the bartender. I tapped her hand to get her attention back to Darcy's request.

"Um. Yeah. Burger and a diet." She shook her head. "That's got to be Joey Breeze's sister. Looks so much like him."

"Two moo-burgers. Poutine or regular fries?"

"Without Gord here," I said with a grin, "I'll go with fries. Don't need the gravy today."

"Same," Courtney added, but her eyes flicked toward the bar again.

"Hey!" I tapped her hand again. "Girlfriend over here, not at the bar."

"Sorry." Courtney took my hand and gave it a squeeze. "I never knew that Joey had a sister."

"Pixie, right? They always have big families."

Courtney nodded and let her eyes drift to the small stage

at the other end of the pub. Darcy had pulled a couple of tables to make room for the platform. The driver of the panel van from outside the bookstore was lifting drums out of travel cases. A long wooden box sat next to the small stage. I had no idea what kind of equipment a band needed, but that box would hold a lot. It was at least a foot tall, six-ish feet long, and a couple of feet wide. Almost like a plain wooden casket.

A tall, hairy creature walked in carrying a long rectangular case and a folding black metal stand. A guitar case was slung over the Sasquatch's shoulder. He'd added a Hawaiian style shirt in a loud print, shorts, and leather sandals over his hairiness.

Beyond him, a short hallway back to the kitchen and, beyond that, the alley had its door propped open. The panel van from earlier was parked just outside.

"Didn't know Darcy had a band coming in," I said, watching as the Sasquatch set the cases on the stage. He jerked the metal stand open into an X shape with a practised flip. He lifted the latches on the rectangular case and removed a bright blue electronic keyboard. It went onto the metal stand.

"It really is college reunion week," Courtney said, shaking her head. "The drummer was in a few of my classes. He liked to hang around Niki and got into one of the male covens. They'd hang out together whenever Greek councils were meeting. Niki and he were on various finance committees together. She was always snooping around anything that smelled of money. Not that he had much, though. Geoff Gage, if I remember his name correctly."

I shook my head. "You remember names from more than a decade ago? And not someone you were close to?"

"Part of my training. You never know when a connection

might matter," Courtney said and moved her eyes to the new bartender walking toward our table. Courtney's eyebrow arched up.

The new girl set our short and fat metal travel tumblers with plastic lids on the table in front of us. She grinned at me. "I hear you're the girl who inspired these cups."

My cheeks reddened. "Yeah. Sorry about that. They're better than cleaning up spills whenever my curse kicks in."

"Oh, no worries, sweetie." She held a hand out. "Zoey Breeze. Great to meet you. Hi Court. Long time, right?"

I shook her hand, but Courtney nodded slowly as a smile settled on her cheeks. "It has been. When did Zoey happen? Are you happy?"

The bartender grinned. "About two years after I left college. I came out to my family once I was sure. Got my legal name changed a year later. Mum knew I was struggling with my identity and insisted I see a counsellor. That really helped me find my true self."

I scrunched my lips sideways, slowly piecing it together. "So, your friend from college didn't have a sister after all?"

Zoey laughed. "Oh, Joey did have a sister. She was hiding inside of him, and it took me a while to realize who I really was."

Courtney smiled, tilting her head slightly. "But are you happy? That's the most important part."

Zoey gave an enthusiastic nod. "Definitely happy."

Darcy stepped in next to Zoey and slid an arm around her waist. "Just like meeting an old friend, right?"

Courtney raised her travel tumbler. "Here's to Zoey!"

"Awww... Thanks!" Zoey blushed, her hair highlight going bright pink in the pixie colour of embarrassment.

Darcy kissed Zoey on the cheek. "I'm happy Zoey found herself, and that she's down here helping me with the bar."

"Let me go check on your burgers," Zoey said, her cheeks glowing red as her hair highlights flared again. "Flag me down if you need anything."

Once she'd popped pixie and darted toward the kitchen, I nodded past Darcy at where the band was setting up. "You starting tourist season early? Usually don't have a band in until May."

"They were playing in Toronto, and I liked their sound." Darcy shrugged. "Figured I'd give them a weekend in Eerie Falls. You all can let me know if they're worth bringing back for a run this summer. Maybe the full eight to twelve weeks if it helps get tourists in."

"Will do," I said with a grin. "They playing tonight?"

"Of course. I'm not paying them to sit here and drink with Bubbles and his biker buddies." She grinned and turned back towards the bar. "Of course, with our new mundane resident, I can't use the magical expansion on the place. Had to warn the band the stage was going to stay small."

"Yeah..." I pointed at the old metal piping and water taps that glowed with an eerie green colour. "I like DeAnn. But... someday I think it would just be easier to tell her about magic so we can stop worrying."

"We'll get by," Darcy added and pointed to the pile of what looked like guitar cases next to the long wooden box. "The guitarist is limited to only two on stage. And that's after I tweaked the enlargement spell to get us another foot wider each week this last month. Figured I'd better sneak up on making the pub larger with our author stopping in daily."

Another pixie darted in from the alley side of the pub. She popped tall behind the keyboard, setting a paper coffee cup, and a bag on top of the keyboard. Gord's Eerie Doughnuts logo of a sheet draped ghost holding a big doughnut seemed to grin at me from the paper sack.

"Hey Suki," the Sasquatch rumbled. "Cords for your keyboard are still in the case."

"Thanks, Randy. In a minute. Sugar first." Her dark hair had light blue highlights, which brightened when she popped one of the ghostly bits, the caramel sugar-coated doughnut holes, into her mouth. She closed her eyes and smiled, her highlights flaring even brighter, almost teal-blue.

The drummer looked up from where he was adding a cymbal to a stand on the left side of the drum kit. That put him right behind the girl.

"She is even more beautiful when her hair lights up," he said, a hint of a French-Canadian accent coming through, but not as well as the creepy stare that accompanied the compliment.

"Stow it, Geoff," Randy the Sasquatch said, a warning in his voice. "Told you before, we have a rule. No dating in the band."

Suki and Randy shared a glance. The pixie ate another doughnut hole, then licked the remaining sugar from her fingers. A moment later, she popped into her pixie form and flew over to the still open case for her keyboard. She pulled one end of a coiled cable and darted over to the sleek and shiny blue keyboard. With practised ease, she slid the shiny metal end into the jack on the keyboard. Another flight to the case, and she pulled the other end of the cord out.

I expected her to fly in a corkscrew and wind the cord around one leg from the centre of the X of the stand. Instead, she gave a practised flip of the cord end, sending it around the metal pipe. She caught it, then flipped it again. Over and over, until the cord trailed off at the stage level. A short flight later, and she plugged it into a junction box Randy had just run to her part of the small stage.

"Talent," I mumbled, watching the pixie girl.

"Hey, girlfriend, over here," Courtney chided me.

My cheeks started burning with embarrassment after getting called out on my own critique of her.

Courtney squeezed my hand and chuckled. "Teasing. But at least I was trying to figure out who Zoey was. I caught you eyeballing the cute new pixie."

"I was just watching her talent with that cord." My cheeks were getting uncomfortably warm by now.

"Umm... hmmmm..." She laughed and raised her cup for a sip. "You ever date a pixie?"

I shook my head and raised my own glass. "What about you?"

"Once, a guy. Back when I was still trying to figure things out," she said, her own cheeks starting to glow pink. "Did you spend any time dating guys?"

I shook my head. "Grams had me figured out early and steered me to girls she thought might return my interest." For once, I was glad that Cleo was spending more time at the shop, rather than riding my hip in her carrier. She hadn't insisted on coming along to make snarky remarks today.

Zoey flew over and popped tall right then. She set a burger in front of Court, then another in front of me.

"Trust me, ladies," she said, "pixie girls are some of the best to date. But stay away from the pixie guys. They love to show off."

Courtney chuckled, nodding. "I found that out. The one I went out with was impressed that he'd learn how to shrink and enlarge body parts."

Zoey nodded. "That's the spell all the pixie guys learn first. I tried to tell my male friends that the girls wouldn't be impressed."

I nodded toward the stage where Darcy leaned on a barstool, one foot up on the lower rung, chatting with Randy, the tall, hairy, Sasquatch. "How about you and Darcy? How'd you meet?"

"She spent most of her Sundays up in Toronto," Zoey said, grinning. "I fell into her eyes right off. Took me a few weeks to get her to notice me. She said she was making sure I wasn't just falling prey to her nature."

"Yeah. Vamps have that allure about them." I blushed, remembering how long I'd pined for Darcy when she first took over this bar. I let my eyes drift back to the stage to avoid looking at Courtney again.

"We spent an entire semester at the Bobbie's law enforcement academy learning about various magical glamours. The vampire one is at the top of the toughest to dodge list."

"Yeah," I nodded. "I fell for it, and Darcy said she wasn't even trying to use it on me. Vamp eyes are tricky."

Back on stage, Suki was at her keyboard tapping buttons, then playing a few notes with her left hand. She popped another ghostly bit into her mouth. Geoff, the drummer, had to slide past her to get up to the drum cases at the front of the stage. The pixie girl gasped, jerked with surprise, and spun. Her hand flashed and slapped him across the face.

The cover of the long wooden case just off that side of the stage flew open on its hinges, and a tall man with flowing white hair surged from within. His long fingers, nails painted an alternating black and blood-red, grasped the drummer by the throat.

A hollow yet loud whisper echoed across the bar's main room. "I warned you. Leave her alone..."

The man turned, holding Geoff over the wooden casket, the drummer's feet dangling in the air.

I gasped. The newcomer's fangs glistened as the vampire leaned in toward Geoff's throat.

3

Darcy appeared out of nowhere, right next to Suki on the stage. Vampire speed. She could make it across the pub in the blink of an eye.

She held out a goblet towards the vampire about to bite Geoff. It was probably full of synthetic red. Looked and tasted just like the real thing, according to vamps, and my undead kitty. Cleo said she only hunted mice to protect our books from their chewing. But I suspected she still had a lot of kitty pounce predator in her nature. Taking over a dead cat had to leave some sort of residual imprint of the host.

Back by the stage, the vamp from the long wooden box turned his gaze slowly toward Darcy.

"Set him down, Marius," the bar owner said in soothing tones. "Drink your fill from the cup."

"He dared to harm Suki," Marius, the new vampire, said in his spooky, loud whisper.

"I'm not hurt, just surprised at getting groped," Suki said, her eyes wide, staring at the vampire.

Marius's eyes darted back to the dangling drummer. Courtney was already on her feet, walking slowly toward the altercation. Darcy noticed her and raised her other hand enough to get Court to stop.

"You're young, Marius." Darcy's voice stayed in a soothing tone. "Waking is always difficult your first few years. Drink first. We'll talk with this man in a few moments when you've broken your fast."

"Marius?" Suki said, reaching out to take the cup from Darcy. She pushed it under Marius's nose. "Please?"

"Bah!" The vamp dropped the drummer. Darcy was fast and caught him under the arms, guiding his body to sit on the edge of the stage. Geoff sucked in a deep breath. Then another. His gaze settled on Courtney, standing with her arms folded.

"I... I want to press charges..." Geoff said and closed his eyes for another gulp of air. "He almost killed me."

"Then I must press charges as well," Suki said with a sigh. "That wasn't the first time you've tried to assault me."

"Sexual assault?" Courtney reached into her back pocket and pulled out her notepad. "That's a very serious charge. Pity we've only got one holding cell here. Your assailant will have to share with Mr. Marius."

"What! I never!" Geoff sputtered, his face going red instead of the pale white it had been.

"My butt wasn't the only part you've grabbed this week," Suki said, planting her hands on her hips. Marius continued sipping from the cup and wisely kept quiet.

Randy the Sasquatch stepped in and set a large hand on Geoff's shoulder. "You didn't really want to press charges against a bandmate, did you? Not a good way to begin your first gig with us."

"I..." Geoff looked back at Marius and shivered, then back at Randy. Despite the seriousness of the situation, I found myself smiling at his aloha shirt and khaki shorts. Not the look I expected from one of our hairy magical cousins.

The drummer shook his head. "No. I won't press charges."

"And..." Randy said, tilting his head to stare at the drummer.

"I'll keep my hands in my pockets around Suki. I don't want another misunderstanding if I brush against her."

Suki's snort showed just how little she believed Geoff's last statement. "If he won't file charges, neither will I."

"You're a good drummer," Randy added, shaking his head. "I didn't want to believe your reputation. You are living up to it, though."

"My reputation of being the best drummer this side of Niagara since Neil Peart?" Geoff said, trying out a joking tone.

Suki and Marius both snorted and rolled their eyes.

Randy shook his shaggy head. "Hardly. I was referring to your wandering hands. Touch Suki again, and you're out. Right then and there. I got basic beats programmed into the keyboard. We'll get along without you like we did when Todd got trampled by the elephant."

His features shifted, and his hairy visage morphed into a human face with a full beard and long, shaggy hair.

A magical chime sounded, and the metal taps with their fake plastic water all around the room flashed red. The mundane alert was active. That explained the auto-illusion spell making Randy appear human.

I glanced toward the front door. DeAnn strolled into the bar. She glanced at the stage, her eyes lingering on the scene there. After a few seconds, she headed my way.

"Oh, Sammi. Mind if I join you?"

"Not at all." I pulled Courtney's plate over so she could sit next to me when she returned. I activated a stasis spell that would keep her food warm while she did her cop glare at Geoff and Marius.

The author sat across from me and pointed toward the stage. "Courtney trying to get into the band?"

"The drummer has wandering hands. Squeezed the girl's butt. The fellow with long white hair grabbed him. Courtney is sorting out if anyone is pressing charges," I said, shaking my head. "Pity. I wanted to hear them play tonight."

"Oh! Not good. They kicking the drummer out? Getting him arrested?" She nodded towards Courtney, still standing by in her uniform.

I shrugged. "No idea. Right before you came in, the tall hairy guy said they would boot the drummer out if he touched Suki, their singer, again."

Zoey wandered over right then. "Hey Sweets, what'll you have?"

DeAnn just chuckled, looking the new girl over. "I haven't been called Sweets in ages. Thanks."

"Zoey is dating Darcy and helping in the bar," I said, trying to work in an introduction. "This is DeAnn Powers, our local *author*." I emphasized the word author as an indicator that she was special, but in a non-magical way.

"Gotcha!" Zoey grinned and nodded, evidently picking up my meaning. With a mundane inside, magical races like pixies and Sasquatches would have their magical shapes blocked or disguised. At least blocked enough, it took a huge effort for a pixie to pop tiny while DeAnn was in the bar.

I pointed towards the stage. "We still get to hear the band tonight?"

Zoey nodded. "Yeah. They'll probably grump at their new drummer for a few hours. I tried to warn Randy when they hired him in Toronto. Geoff has very talented hands, or so he believes. He was slapped by several girls, both staff and patrons, at my last gig. But the owner knew his family and smoothed things over for him."

"If he's got a reputation," I shook my head, "why'd they hire him?"

Zoey blew a breath and shrugged. "I have no clue. I took a day off to get my stuff packed up to move down here. When I showed up, Darcy said she'd hired Suki and Randy to play a week here. I thought they were still searching for a replacement for Todd, poor fellow."

DeAnn tilted her head. "Oh, did they lose someone?"

"Todd was their last drummer. They had a gig playing at one of the country clubs, out on the patio. In one of those big white tents. The ballroom inside was for special events like weddings." Zoey shook her head and sighed. "A couple from India was having their wedding there. That day, the groom rode in on an Elephant. So cool!"

DeAnn grinned. "Yes! I've always wanted to see an Indian wedding in person. So regal!"

"Well, after the groom was delivered, some idiot on the eighteenth green decided to chip a few golf balls at the beast." Zoey closed her eyes, then blew out a breath. "Good weather for one week, and that idiot just had to be out golfing. Todd saw the beast get riled up and charge at the pavilion tent. He tried to distract the elephant and keep it from trampling a bunch of guests. Poor fellow ended up in a full body cast. It's going to be years before he plays the drums again."

"Oh, that's terrible!" DeAnn pressed a hand to her mouth.

"What happened to the elephant? I mean they didn't kill him, did they?"

Courtney slid back into the booth, sitting next to me and raised an eyebrow. "The one that got loose in Toronto, trampled a tent, and that poor drummer? It's been placed at a zoo. The golfer that goaded it, however, is on the hook for damages. He tried to blame the animal handlers. They found five balls at the scene, all the brand the golfer bragged about always using. Said all five bounced off the elephant's face. One hitting it right in the eye."

"Ow!" DeAnn and I both said.

She nodded. "I'd want to trample that golfer if he hit me in the eye with a golf ball."

"Did you get them sorted out?" I pointed at the stage while Courtney took another bite from her burger.

"Randy, the... tall, hairy one did," she said in between bites. "Thanks for waiting for me."

"Just looking out for my girlfriend, the constable. She's always on duty."

Courtney flashed me a grin and nibbled on a few fries.

"What will you have, sweetie?" Zoey asked DeAnn. "I came over for your order and got sidetracked."

"Oh! How about a mango-thingie!"

"Mango-thingie?" Zoey cocked an eyebrow. "Never mind. I'll ask Darcy."

"Mango juice, white rum, and something," I said with a shrug. "Darcy whipped it up a couple of months ago for DeAnn."

The author nodded. "Found it at a resort down in Florida. But I couldn't remember the exact name. Darcy's is better than what I had at the resort."

Once Zoey headed over to the bar, I glanced back at the

stage. Randy, Suki, and the pale Marius were close together, talking in whispers. Geoff the drummer, nowhere to be seen.

"Did they fire the drummer?" I asked Courtney.

She shook her head, popping the last of the burger in her mouth. After she finished it, she nodded towards the alley. "He's out for a smoke. They're deciding if he gets his walking papers today or another chance."

"So, you don't have to arrest anyone?" DeAnn asked. "You had your serious face on when I walked in. I thought for sure one of them was going out in cuffs."

"It's always a good day when I don't have to use the cuffs," Courtney said.

The alley door banged shut, and Geoff strode in, propped a foot on the stage, and leaned forward. "Well?" The drummer's question was almost a demand and loud enough to travel across the room.

"One last chance," Randy proclaimed, his voice slightly softer than Geoff's but not by much. "One more grabbing, groping, or unwanted touch of any girl, and I'll toss you into the street myself."

"It's a long walk back to Toronto," Suki said, crossing her arms and glaring at him.

"With your drums," Marius added. "I will aim for your head when I fling them out the door after you. Then I'll toss out the cases."

"I knew you'd see it my way," Geoff said with a big grin. He spun and stepped over to the bar. "Hey, sweetheart, give me pint of your best IPA."

Zoey flashed him a polite smile and filled a glass from a tap behind the bar.

"Oh..." Courtney muttered under her breath, staring at the front door. I turned to follow her gaze.

Lorne and Niki walked in from outside.

"Constable, when you're finished with your lunch," Lorne said, his voice in a stoic, official tone but still overemphasized the woman's honorific. "Mizz Durand needs to spend time shadowing you on your rounds. She'll be here a few days. Since my vacation begins tomorrow, you'll be her main contact."

Courtney stiffened slightly and gave a brusk nod. "Of course, Sergeant Pebblebrook." Evidently she was going to be all formal and use Lorne's title while this Niki girl was in town.

"Excellent. I could use a few hours of downtime this afternoon, since I have evening call," Lorne said and nodded toward the stage. "With the new band opening tonight, it should be quiet in town until they stop and all the bar patrons drift home. Since they're all locals, they should behave and save me the trouble of writing reports right before my fishing trip."

Niki stared at the stage. Randy and Marius were rearranging the gear. Geoff's drum kit had already been moved to the side nearest Marius's wooden casket. Several metal stands propped up what I assumed were the vampire's guitars. Randy's bass guitars were lined up right behind Suki's keyboard. That had been pushed even farther away from the drum kit, which was a pity. If Suki were the lead singer, I'd want her in the centre as much as possible. But I understood why Geoff and his wandering hands were relegated to being as far away from Suki as possible.

Niki's eyes darted back to Courtney. "Constable? I'd like to get moving, so I can make notes for my report. And I want to be done in time to catch the band tonight."

"Of course, Mizz Durand." Courtney rose. Her face stayed

in her stoic cop expression. Actually, it was more of a lack of an expression. "Or am I supposed to use your Special Assistant title?"

"Either works, Constable," Niki said with a slight smile. Her tone was more akin to ordering household staff around than greeting an old college friend.

4

DeAnn and my bestie Gord McKenna, son of the owner of Eerie Donuts, sat with me at one of the four-top tables in the centre of Eerie Taps. The band was going to play in about half-an-hour. I was getting concerned enough that I kept checking my phone for a text from Courtney. But not concerned enough to actually text her myself.

Gord leaned back in his seat, feet propped up on what would be Courtney's chair next to me. Most of the tables were filled, and we didn't want to lose the seat before my girlfriend arrived.

"Oh, is this seat taken?" Niki smiled and rested a hand on the chair back.

"Sorry," I said with a nod. "It is."

Well, if Niki was here alone, that meant that Court was probably changing out of her uniform and would be here shortly. Close enough.

"I'm sure that Courtney won't mind if I join you." Niki's

tone dripped with politeness. My girlfriend might have to be polite to her old rival, but I didn't have to.

"Sorry. I'm waiting on my date for tonight." I smiled back at her.

Niki raised an eyebrow, her smile slowly fading.

"I see... Miss Cupertino, is it?" Her eyes stayed on mine. "There isn't anything in this world I can't get if I want it."

"Oh," Gord's voice cut in. "Could you get me a strawberry milkshake? The ice cream shop isn't open for the summer yet, and I'm jonesing for a shake."

Niki stared at Gord for a moment. He returned her stare with innocent puppy dog eyes.

"I see..." Niki spun on her designer heel and headed towards the bar. A stool was open next to Bubbles and the space where the servers stood waiting on Darcy to get their drink orders. Zoey was walking between the tables, heading back that way.

"Aren't you mister spicy?" I said with a chuckle. "Way to distract and stick up for me and Courtney."

"Well, if Courtney isn't happy, then you're not happy." Gord grinned back at me. "Besides, after you described her history, I really didn't want to sit with her."

"That one." DeAnn tipped her head toward Niki at the bar. "If this were a murder mystery, I'd write her as the main perp. Or at least the front running red herring. She might even be a victim. The one everyone loves to hate."

Up at the bar, the special assistant to the MPP was pointedly ignoring Bubbles, our local hairy-scary biker werebear. That meant she was looking toward the order station between the two, curved, brass poles when Zoey stepped up to place her table's orders. Niki's eyes went wide for a second.

Zoey smiled at her, and they seemed to have a polite

conversation. But when Darcy set several drinks on Zoey's tray, the pixie girl nodded and smiled at Niki, then turned away. Her smile dropped the instant her back faced Niki. Zoey noticed my gaze and rolled her eyes with a slight head tilt back toward Niki.

I felt a hand on my shoulder and Courtney leaned in. I kissed her. Gord dropped his feet from the chair so Court could sit with us.

"You survived your ordeal." I grinned and slid her metal tumbler of wine towards her.

"Not by much. And I get two more days of shepherding her around since Lorne is off on a fishing trip tomorrow." Courtney pried the plastic top off the tumbler, swirled the wine, and inhaled its aroma. "Mmmm. Got me the good stuff."

"Figured you'd need it after your afternoon."

She took a sip, then another. "Two more days of her. That's all I have to worry about."

"What exactly is her title?" DeAnn asked, leaning forward. "I'm still trying to learn all about the provincial government."

"Well," I said, not sure how to translate the fae minister and his staff into mundane speak. "She's some sort of special assistant to an MPP. Outside of a few key positions, the ministers can give out positions however they like."

"Special assistant..." DeAnn said, letting that title roll around for a few seconds. "Yep. She's definitely victim status. I'd better pay closer attention to her. The new book I'm writing needs a good victim that everyone hates. That Niki whatshername sounds like a prime candidate."

"Do you do that often?" Gord asked, leaning forward to sip from the straw jutting from his tall travel tumbler. "Write people you've met into your books?"

"All the time." DeAnn grinned. "Oh, names are changed to protect the innocent and the guilty."

"Oh... well, if you put me in a book, can I be taller?" Gord grinned at her, flashing a cheesy grin with one eyebrow raised.

DeAnn giggled. "Of course. Would you like to be a visiting detective? Always a ladies' man? The entire town swooning over you?"

"What? No. Yuck!" Gord shook himself. "I'd rather be the tech guy. Looking stuff up for the detective. But taller. With good friends."

Courtney chuckled, scooting her chair closer, so she could lean back into my shoulder.

"How'd the day with Mizz Special Assistant go?" I dreaded to ask but figured she'd need to vent.

Courtney took the cap off the wine cup and tilted it back, almost draining it.

"That well, huh?"

She took a deep breath, then closed her eyes. "She is only in town for two more days."

"You'll survive," I said, running my hand across her shoulders.

"Oh! They're getting ready." DeAnn pointed toward the stage. Randy the Sasquatch had a bass guitar draped from a strap that crossed his bright green aloha shirt. Of course, with the mundane detector glaring red, Randy looked more human than squatchy. Suki stepped up onto the stage, helped with a courteous hand from silver haired Marius. Geoff the drummer stepped carefully behind Randy, over cords and past sound gear to shimmy sideways into his place behind the drum kit on the small stage.

We were treated to a few minutes of listening to "Test... test... can you hear me in the cheap seats?" And "Check,

check... Credit Card..." from Randy, Marius, and Suki. Evidently Geoff was drums only, no vocals.

"Everyone good on drinks?" Zoey asked, sliding between tables and pausing by us.

"Another cup of red wine, please?" Courtney asked.

"Two," I said. DeAnn and Gord added their own drinks as well.

"Good evening, Eerie Falls," Suki's voice echoed from the speakers right as Zoey headed up to the bar. "I'm Suki, and these are the Sasquatches." The three gents all wore aloha shirts and pressed khaki pants, similar to Randy's. Marius's was in a blood red colour on a field of black. Geoff's was more lively with blues and yellows.

"Speak for yourself," Marius interjected with a well-rehearsed line. "Only one of us is tall and hairy."

Randy's long fingers banged out a bass riff on his strings. "Who, me?"

Suki let her fingers drift across her keyboard, adding playfully to the bass line Randy laid down. She wore a feminine cut aloha shirt in teal and pinks, with a white skirt short enough to show off her legs, but long enough to stay modest on the stage.

By now, Geoff and Marius added to the tune, and they were off with a standard rock song from the eighties. Smiles on the bar patrons grew, and we quieted to enjoy the music.

About six songs into the set, while we tapped our feet or hands to the rhythm, they slowed their beat and Suki waved a hand toward the drum kit. "That's Geoff Gage on the skins."

He launched into a cacophony of beats and rolling thunder from his kit. Non-musical me shook my head in awe.

"He's good," Gord said, almost shouting to be heard over the short solo.

"Going to run down to the school and get your old bass drum?" I shot him a teasing smile.

"Only if they're going to play some Fleetwood Mac," Gord said and grinned. "My marching band uniform doesn't fit any longer, though."

"And Marius Rapp on lead guitar."

The vampire let his fingers fly. Based on Darcy's comments earlier, I suspected he was still a young vamp. But he showed the speed of the undead. His fingers were a blur, yet the notes were enticing, each distinct. They blended into a haunting melody that seemed to tug at my inner soul.

As he wrapped up, Suki waved toward the tall bassist. "The hairy Randy Mueller on bass."

The Sasquatch again laid down some bass riffs that I recognized from three different songs, each progressing into the next. He leaned into his mic. "And Suki Yoshino, the cute one, on keys and lead vocals."

Suki let her fingers dance over her keys.

"I'm glad to see you all came in from the sprawling subdivisions to enjoy our music."

She shot Randy a glance, and her notes morphed the free form melody into one familiar to most Canadians who followed the local boys in Rush. The almost haunting notes were joined by Randy's bass and beats from Geoff's drums.

I wasn't musically inclined, but mentally sang along with the lyrics. Following the *geometric order,* and *insulated border,* even Gord was tapping out the drumbeat and mouthing the words...*shopping malls.* When Suki sang the finale, *the restless dreams of youth,* we all applauded.

"Ugh!" Gord groaned over the applause. "Love that song but hate the memories of high school it brings back."

Randy kept the prog-rock theme going, launching into the

rhythm of *Tom Sawyer*. After that, Marius took over with the opening riff of *Limelight*. After that Suki, tapped some settings on her keyboards, and yet another well know intro, this time a recorded synth line started. Her fingers added the beat on the keys. Bah... ba-bah. *"Out here in the fields..."* A classic from The Who.

Marius did a wonderful Pete Townshend impression, his tall, lithe form reminiscent of the rocker from the 1980s, bouncing around the stage, swinging his arm in a huge wind-mill to send the power chord stroke echoing from the amps.

The song's finale, instead of a harmonica, was voiced by Suki's fingers across her keyboard. She had shifted the settings to mimic the classic Daltrey solo on the mouth organ. Marius bounced, Geoff pounded out an increasing tempo on the drums. Only Randy was stoic, his fingers dancing across the bass strings. The final beats of the classic prog-rock song were punctuated by another windmill from Marius.

The sound of strings snapping wasn't the classic end to the song. His pick tumbled from the guitarist's fingers and sailed into the crowd. The silly undead guy must have forgotten his strength.

Randy's eyes went wide, but he pounded out a familiar riff and sang, "Another one bites the dust! Or was it more than one string?"

"All six, and his favourite guitar," Suki replied, while Geoff launched into a surf-rock drum solo. Randy leaned into his mic and cackled with laughter. He used a falsetto voice to pronounce, "Wipeout!"

Marius had all six strings pulled from his guitar. He flung them off stage, over toward the bar. If he weren't a vamp, he wouldn't have gotten that far, that fast. But if he didn't have undead strength, he wouldn't have wiped out six strings at once.

Geoff trailed off on his solo, looking at Randy, who picked up the melody of Queen's classic bass line. We, in the audience, started clapping along.

After a moment, Marius turned back, all six strings replaced. He grabbed another of his blood red picks from the contraption on his mic stand.

"Wow! He was fast..." DeAnn's voice called out her surprise.

"Musicians have to be," Gord said, trying to give a plausible explanation.

"We'll call this our first set," Randy said. "Someone needs to tune that axe. Remember to tip your servers, folks. We'll be back in fifteen."

Darcy and her girls got busy, taking and filling drink orders. Zoey and two other girls, both pixies, moved through the tables, writing orders. Darcy had even pulled Bubbles behind the bar to help mix drinks.

Geoff headed toward the bar while Suki and Randy headed to the alley. Marius stayed on stage, his ear cocked, tightening the tuning pegs.

Zoey slid between the drummer, who was trying to chat up Niki. She rolled her eyes and headed toward the hallway where the restrooms waited. Geoff turned toward Zoey, reaching out. Her hand intercepted his with practised ease and pushed it toward the brass pole marking the boundary of the server station at the bar.

"That one better be careful," Courtney said, shaking her head. "Someone's boyfriend or daddy is going to teach him a lesson."

5

utside, a train whistle sounded, and the squeal of brakes and thunk of rail cars banging and slowing intruded on my aching brain. Cleo pawed my nose.

"Leave me alone!" I pulled the pillow over my head.

Your girlfriend is already up, showered and gone.

"Ugh... not another morning..."

Did you listen to me before you went to that show? I told you not to drink so much wine.

The pillow didn't muffle the sound of her voice. That was the downside of having a telepathic cat.

"You told me that *after* I drank the wine." Through the fog in my brain, I questioned that as soon as I mumbled it. Maybe she had told me before I left to meet DeAnn and Gord at the bar?

Cleo didn't respond. She just poked my forehead again with a paw. This time, there was a hint of claws coming through.

"All right!" I tossed the pillow off and rolled carefully out of bed. "I'm up. Just not functional."

Twenty minutes later, I was in the kitchen, without makeup, but clean and dressed. "They may just get my normal face today..." I mumbled as I pushed the on-button for the teakettle. Fortunately, Court had filled it with water and set out my travel tumbler and favourite morning tea.

Has the constable spoken to her landlord about getting out of her lease yet?

My head was in my hands, elbows on the breakfast bar. "I'm not pushing her to move in." Definitely a hair in a pony-tail day. I didn't even want to try a make-up application spell this morning.

She's here four or five times a week. Cleo's mental chuckle echoed in my head. *She's even added a safe for her firearm in your closet. You two are practically living together now.*

"Not officially." I kept my eyes closed and rubbed both sides of my head at the temples. My phone chimed. I glanced at my wrist. Yep, smart watch was there but upside down. How did I do that? I had no mental energy for reading upside-down words. After sliding the watch off, then back on with the correct orientation, I pried an eye open again.

"Great. The faerock delivery is arriving this morning. Another trip I have to make today."

Arrived, you mean. That was the train pulling in behind the town hall. You need to get your grandfather's order too, dear. Faerock is what recharges magic and spells. We both know your grandfather let most of the spells on the bookshop dwindle to almost nothing. Without the faerock, you'll have to use all of your own magical energy to recharge the spells. And you aren't that strong, yet, dear. You'd best get the faerock orders.

I sighed and looked at Cleo through one eye, trying to

ignore the pressure in my head. The kettle clicked off, so I poured water and lowered my tea bag into the tumbler. I was careful, quietly wishing my klutz curse to leave me alone for a few more minutes, and got the lid pressed on the tumbler without dumping scalding hot water over me and the counter. After that, I leaned forward, resting my head on my folded arms.

A tingle of magic made the hairs on my arms stand up. I cracked an eye open and stared at Cleo's paw on my tumbler.

A cure I learned to use whenever Merlin sat with Rhodri Reece. The Lieutenant Colonel's stories could be long winded and leave your grandfather with nothing to do but drink while they wound on and on.

I remembered Rhodri, most recently, from my time in Misty Valley. He could definitely tell a story. No wonder Grams had a hangover cure spell in her memorized arsenal.

I took a sip of my tea, closing my eyes and letting the warmth spread through me. I wasn't sure if it was the tea's temperature or Cleo's spell, but that feeling nibbled at the edges of my headache. Three sips later and my head was almost normal again.

Drink it all or you'll crash halfway through the day. You'll need extra sleep eventually, though. That cure can only do so much before your body has to catch up.

"Yes, ma'am," I said and poured a bit of the bottle of vampire red I kept in the fridge for her to lick from her dish.

Taking the tumbler with me into the bedroom, I actually felt good enough to try a makeup spell and to add a little style to my hair. I might have lunch with Courtney if her day stayed quiet. It was nice to have a special someone I could look good for.

Fifteen minutes later, Cleo sat by the door, waiting for me. This time, she ignored the open cat carrier.

"I thought your paws were too delicate for the cold ground."

Cleo glanced at me, raising one kitty eyebrow, then returned to licking her right front paw.

"Suit yourself. First stop, Eerie Doughnuts."

Drink all of your tea dear. Especially if you want to go see the band again tonight. It has a downslope throughout the day. The more you drink today, the gentler the slope is.

"Suki said they're doing songs from the 50s and 60s tonight," I said, pulling the door open then locking it behind us. "That's more your and Gramps's speed."

Really, dear. Merlin and I were already dating and adventuring when Mozart was writing his first sonata. She trotted along beside me on the walk into town. *We requested his help on figuring out a musical puzzle on one tomb. He must have remembered part of the puzzle even after I hit him with a forget-it spell. His dissonance quartet was definitely inspired by the notes we had to play to get past that spell lock.*

By the time we made our way to Eerie Doughnuts, I finished my tea and was able to toss the teabag in the bin. With the headache totally gone now, I passed my cup to Gord at the counter.

"You're late today."

I chuckled. "At least I got up and put my face on. You look like you do whenever you get a hot new video game and stay up all night playing it."

Drake Huppe snorted and rose from his table. "At first, I thought old Gord-o might have found a date. Maybe that new chick at Eerie Taps hadn't heard how boring he is."

"Stuff it Huppe," Gord growled.

That made Drake laugh as he pulled on his jacket. He wore a ball cap with an embroidered logo of his old minor league hockey club, the Fort Erie Rumbling Trolls. "I heard Darcy hired a new pixie. She needs to see what a real man looks like if she's new in town. I'll stop in for lunch today."

I shook my head and repressed a chuckle. "Trust me, Drake, Zoey is so not your type."

"Why wouldn't she be? Oh, you thinking about dumping Constable Crazy and dating the new girl?"

"Shove it, Huppe." I crossed my arms, staring at him. "And Zoey is dating Darcy. You can try to get them to split. It'll be interesting to see what Darcy does to you when she finds out."

Huppe rolled his eyes. "Another lesbian? We need more girls in Eerie Falls. Sounds like I'll have to go to Timmie's for lunch then."

I didn't uncross my arms, nor take my eyes off the town jerk. "I'm sure the girls on staff there are anxiously awaiting your imminent return." Huppe and his arrogance brought back a nagging little part of my headache, so I let the snark drip off my words. He deserved it.

A touch more sarcasm wouldn't have hurt. Cleo's mental chuckle echoed in my brain. *If he weren't leaving, I'd go catch a mouse and leave it in his truck's cab. He deserves that, too.*

Huppe just grinned and tapped his hat in a mock salute.

"Later, Klutz-girl. Let me know when you want to start dating for real." He pulled the door open and exited before I could reply.

I glanced down at Cleo. "Mouse. Definitely."

She looked up from her never-ending task of licking her paw. *I shall see to it the next time we encounter him.*

Gord passed me my cup and set the bag of doughnut holes

on the counter next to the pay tablet. "Ma said I need to go get the faerock order this morning. Want to walk down with me?" He tapped my order into the till and swivelled the pad towards me.

I tapped it with my wand to pay. "Yeah. If I can get Gramps to come in and watch the shop by then. I'd better call Betty and see if he's at her place."

"Isn't he there most nights?"

I nodded. "She's started doing his laundry. And even made him buy more socks."

"I thought you'd been stealing his socks?"

Cleo's mental chuckle cut into my thoughts. *You should have passed them to her as soon as you knew they were serious.*

"Well, I only took one or two at a time, so I knew when he was about to get swallowed by his piles of dirty laundry. Betty appreciated my system when I explained it to her. But wasn't thrilled with the extra dozen mismatched socks I gave her to work back in. What time are you going to get the faerock?"

"Probably be about ten. I'll stop in and see if you got your grandfather moving."

An hour later, I had the shop open, and Betty had Gramps up and moving. I worked on filling a few orders we had come in via the web while I waited on ten o'clock to roll around. G'Rex had finished our addition to the shop. My new office was roomier and actually had a table I'd managed to keep mostly clear of books. There was enough room to set up a station for wrapping, weighing, and adding postage labels to our outgoing parcels.

I heard the door chime sound and headed out to find Gord in one of the easy chairs we kept for those who felt the urge to read before purchasing.

"Ready, Sammi?"

"Just about," I said and watched Gramps push open the front door. "The relief shift has arrived."

"Let me get some coffee before you leave, Sammi," he said, heading toward the office to hang up his hat.

"Coffee is fresh," I called after him. "Packages are ready for the post. On the shipping table."

"So I noticed," Gramps said, returning and handing me two notecards, each with a name and number scrawled on them. Well, the one with Merlin Cupertino was scrawled. Betty's was much neater and very legible. "Will you be a dear and get my faerock orders too? I might take Betty out for an evening. It's been a while since I've fed my infernal in the sedan."

"No problem, Gramps." I grabbed one of the magical shopping bags we kept behind the counter. It wasn't a surprise that he hadn't fed the demonic critter in his car. The Infernal brand engines, like most fae machines, used infernals to generate heat, and convert it into whatever kind of energy the machine needed. "Do you mind if I grab lunch while we're out?"

"Not at all." He sat in the chair Gord had just vacated, setting his coffee on the small table between the chairs and unfolded the Fort Erie Times newspaper. That was a fae-run paper, and a moving photo of the gambling boat that sailed Lake Erie showed the luxury boat bobbing as it approached the dock. The headline read "Tourist season to begin! *Tisserand* ready to sail."

"Taking her out on the gambling boat?" I said half in jest. Who knew what my grandfather was thinking of?

"Perhaps. Neither of us gamble, so it would be more for dinner and a tour of the lake."

"Come on, Sammi." Gord pulled the door open. "I told Ma I'd be back to help with the lunch rush."

Outside, we saw Zoey exit the side door of Eerie Taps and start heading the same direction. She noticed us and waited for us at the corner where we crossed the street to her side.

"Darcy said town hall is this way?" She pointed up the street.

Gord nodded. "Yep. Faerock order?"

"Yeah. The joy of dating the undead. They try to avoid sunlight." Zoey's long legs kept up with Gord, and I had to walk faster to keep up with both of them.

"Slow down, you two!" I called a step behind.

"Sorry Sammi," Gord said, his face flushing.

Town hall already had a bit of a queue. We became numbers seven to nine as we joined the line. The rail cars behind the building were boxcars.

Mrs. Gerards already had her check-out station set up. The next patron stepped up. She checked them off her list and passed an order card to the gnome next to her. He trotted back to the rail car and passed the ticket to another gnome set up under one of the pop-up pavilion tents.

The other gnome read the order ticket and pulled a bright green sack of the faerock from the open door of the boxcar behind him. Even the inside of the boxcar glowed with a green faerock residue, as did the dozen similar cars behind it. To a mundane, they'd just see a dirty old boxcar, maybe forty or fifty feet in length. But to fae, we could see the residual magic that leached into the cars.

The gnome under the canopy carefully poured glowing green pellets from the bag onto a brass scale, the type with a platform on either side. He added a small weight to the other platform. He then dipped a pair of tongs into the bag and added a single green pellet to the scale. The platforms balanced. He dumped the faerock on the scale into a much smaller bag that glowed with its own protection spell. Faerock magic was potent and concentrated. The stuff formed when magic from ley lines leeched into the rock surrounding the magical channels that ran through the Earth.

"Fresh from St. Maurice," the first gnome declared, returning to our queue and passing the bag over to the patron. She took it gingerly and frantically thrust it into her magical shopping bag.

"Don't worry, miss," the gnome said. "Our protection bags have top-notch spells on them. No danger of leakage. And don't keep it out too long. Our bags will protect you. If you start laughing uncontrollably, you've had too much exposure."

Despite his assurances, I still worried. Faerock in its raw form is nasty stuff.

He and Mrs. Gerards glanced up at the person in front of us.

Zoey repressed a shiver. "Bah! Faerock. I've heard too many horror stories of pixies with birth defects because a vein of faerock got exposed close to their communities."

"That's why they use the green protection bags, dear," Mrs. Gerards said, and slid a pamphlet to Zoey. "Here's all the warnings and proper handling instructions. Do be careful. Don't want you to lose your wings."

The gnome was speedy. Another dump from the big green bag. A pellet or two added to balance the scales. Another smaller bag of faerock was passed over. We were in front of Mrs. Gerards in no time and let Zoey go first. She passed over Darcy's and the Eerie Taps id numbers.

"Oh, you're the new girl. So nice to meet you!" Mrs.

Gerards said, resting her knitting back in her lap as she checked the list on her tablet.

A moment later, the gnome passed a large bag of faerock over, followed by a smaller one. "Don't go pixie, miss," he warned Zoey. "Faerock doesn't like to be shrunk."

"Hmmm. I didn't know that," Gord said, rubbing his chin with a thoughtful expression creeping onto his face. "What happens if it is?"

The gnome pressed his hands together, then flicked his fingers wide and spread his hands. "Boom!"

6

"I don't wanna go boom!" Zoey said but grinned. "Don't worry. All young pixies get the faerock lectures every year in school."

"You can put the rock in magical storage. You can spit on it. You can feed it to an infernal," the gnome said, his voice settling into a well-practised lecture tone. "Just don't shrink it. The gnomes at the processing plant in St. Mo already compacted it as far as we dare. Do you need a refresher on how to load the rock and not be exposed?"

"Thanks, I've got the instructions here to use." She waved the pamphlet.

"Those are good things to know," Gord said, giving a slow nod. "Not that I'd ever had a need to shrink faerock. I just want to get the order back to the doughnut shop and feed the infernals that run our ovens."

"Don't forget to fuel your cars," I added.

Gord shrugged. "Mom rarely drives. I checked the fuel

gauge. Dust from the shop's bag should keep her car's infernal happy until fall."

By now, Mrs. Gerards had Gord's three orders checked off. The bags the gnome passed over were about the same size as the ones Zoey got. The infernals in his doughnut ovens and fryers must like a lot of faerock.

Gord dropped the bags into his backpack, and I stepped up to Mrs. Gerards' desk.

"Sammi, Eerie Tomes, and..." Mrs. Gerards let the list trail off with a questioning tone.

"And Merlin Cupertino. And Betty Grindlespool." I passed over the card with the numbers Gramps had handed to me as we left.

A moment later, I had four smaller bags, each with an order number stamped on them. Fortunately, electricity was provided by our power plant under the town hall building. We still called the fees we paid to the town the "hydro bill" like the rest of Canada. But our hydro was really an infernal, happily munching on faerock, and giving off heat to turn the boilers that made electricity. I suspected several huge bags of faerock would make their way to the cellar to feed the infernals there.

"Ugh. Now I need to work on our shop's protection spells," I grumbled, dropping the faerock packages into my purse. I didn't want to risk magical storage after the lecture we'd just received.

The bags were for fuelling our vehicles and for reinforcing our main enchantments. Cleo had reminded me to increase our standing order so she and I could rebuild our shop's book golem.

"Just don't let DeAnn see the book Golem in your shop," Gord said.

Zoey turned my way, her eyes wide. "Book golem?"

"Protection guardian over our shop. Grams and Gramps constructed it." I shrugged, not sure I'd be able to figure it out without Cleo's help. "Gramps had let the golem and protection spells in our shop die out over the last decade or two after Grams passed."

Gord laughed. "Yeah, and that golem came in handy a few months ago. Even if you said he was all rag-tag and falling apart."

Zoey shook her head but had an underlying chuckle. "Poor fellow. You need to give him some Dickens and Chaucer. I want to see your book golem. Does he smite interlopers while quoting Shakespeare?" She dropped her voice into a false bass tone. "Alas, poor interloper! I knew him, Horatio, a fellow of infinite thieving, of most repugnant larceny, he hath broken in too many times, and now, how abhorred in my sight he is! My fist crushes him."

"Oh! Most excellent!" My smile grew listening to Zoey's impromptu changes in the lines. "Did you study theatre?"

Zoey nodded. "I kept trying out for female roles and got quite a few. And I was the understudy for Hamlet in my third year at university."

"Were you out then?" I asked.

Zoey shook her head. "No, but I was dreaming of it. There was a silent film made in Germany back in the 1920s, where Asta Nielsen played Hamlet. They altered the plot to show Hamlet as a girl who was raised as a boy. And she's not the only actor to have played the lead as female. Many stage productions have cast women as the prince of Denmark. That would be a dream gig."

"Well, if you head over to Stratford, they've got a Shake-speare Festival," Gord added.

"Yeah," I nodded. "Love going to the shows there. The artistic directors are always looking for a new approach to redo the Bard's plays in an interesting way."

"I thought about it but never made the drive," Zoey said, with a minor shrug and head tilt. "Besides, I've got a bar to run and a cute Irish lass to kiss. No time for the stage right now."

A pixie zipped past us at head level. "Hi Gord, hi Sammi, and hi new person," Willard called.

"Must be time for his late morning doughnut," Gord said, and turned to cross the street at the corner. "Better run. If Willard is there for his second doughnut, Ma is about to change over for the lunch. I gotta get back."

"Bye Gord," I called as he jogged across the street. I figured I'd keep walking with Zoey and duck into Taps for an early lunch since Gramps had the shop.

Zoey glanced off toward the doughnut shop, where Willard popped tall and pulled the door open. "Hmmm. I should go out and introduce myself to the Pixie Elder council here. The councils always like to know when a new pixie moves into their town."

"Well, one of the council elders just zipped past. Just don't get between Willard and his doughnut. Nice guy, though. Unless..." I trailed off, thinking of the last few times we'd actually chatted. He'd been around in an official capacity then.

"Unless what?" Zoey asked. We passed the front door to Taps, and she kept walking toward the alley at the far side.

"He's the town EMS. All of it. He showed up when DeAnn and I found the body in the alley next to the doughnut shop. He was still nice, but professional."

"You've only got one pixie as a medic in this town?"

49

"Well, Eerie Falls isn't big. We go to Port Rowan or Fort Erie if we need medical aid."

"Isn't London closer?" Zoey cocked her head and looked off to the north-west.

"It is but doesn't have a strong fae presence." I gave a shrug. "Fort Erie is a border town with the crossing into the U.S. They've got a bigger Bobbie presence there, so more fae are in that area. Even the local paper up there has a fae edition."

Zoey turned the corner and led me into the alley, then behind the building. Darcy's big black SUV was parked here, as was the van that Suki and her band drove. Randy, in his full hairy appearance, leaned against the wall, a cigar clenched between his teeth, and the Fort Erie Times folded down. He had a pen in hand and was working on the crossword.

"Morning, Randy," Zoey called. "Faerock train is in at city hall if you need to fuel up the van."

"Just did that in Toronto. We should be good for another month. The inside-enlarge enchantment sucks a lot of the juice out of a bag of faerock, though. That is the one nice thing about Geoff. He knew enough about making insides larger than they should be. Said his family works in the cauldron business. He showed Suki how to add some enhancements to our van's enlarge spells."

"I wondered how you got Marius's casket and Geoff's drums to fit in there," Zoey said, nodding. "Makes sense. When I was in college, the bands I hung out with never had the spare looneys for an inside-enlarge spell. The best they could do was shrink their gear down."

"That never works for long," Randy said and tucked the paper under his arm. "Strings go out of tune, and drums hate to be shrunk. Too much tension on the skins."

Zoey laughed. "One drummer I knew ended up inside his bass drum after their shrink spell wore out on a road trip. Must be nice to have the extra room in there."

"It's not much, but it's home on the road." Randy waved toward the van. "Wanna see? It's nothing but gear storage in the back. But we got a mini-kitchen up front, in case we need a hot meal while travelling."

"Let me feed Darcy's car," Zoey said and pulled out the smaller of her faerock bags. She held it out at arm's length on her walk over to Darcy's vehicle. She passed me the pamphlet. "Would you hold this open? I value my wings and don't want to lose them because I skipped a step."

"Sure," I said, but being around faerock, even in the protection bags, made me a tad nervous too.

It didn't take her long to open Darcy's SUV and feed the smaller bag of faerock into the fuel port. The car seemed to sigh, and a puff of brimstone burped from the tailpipe. Me and Randy both stepped back, waving our hands to clear the stench. Leaving the other bag of faerock on the roof of the car, Zoey popped pixie and darted back, out of the stench.

"Cauldrons! They always amaze me. The air is clearer over here," Randy said and nodded toward the side of the van.

"You mean how they shrink a big old powerful snarling infernal down into a teeny-tiny living space?" I grinned at the movie reference. Randy chuckled.

"Exactly." He tapped his wand on the side door of the van and pulled it open. They were the French style van doors. One swung open to the right, then another opened left and made a wide opening. The front section looked normal, but behind the seats, another twenty feet of space existed in what should have been a mere five feet. But that wasn't what caught our eyes.

Randy jerked upright and stepped back. Behind the hair that cascaded down over his brow, his eyes went wide. "What?! Not again! We lost another drummer. Poor Geoff. Who'd want to do that to him?"

I shifted my gaze and stared past his shoulder, into the second row of seats. Right behind the driver's seat, Geoff the drummer sat in one of the captain-style bucket seats that was rotated to face the side door. And he was dead, his mouth open, his face frozen and discoloured. He still wore the same clothing as at the show. But his belt was undone, and his aloha shirt untucked and totally unbuttoned. His hands, balled into fists, sat in his lap.

My phone was in my hand, and I pressed it to my ear. I instinctively dialled.

"Constable Montrose," Courtney's voice was professional. That meant she was probably with that Niki woman.

"Um... I'd like to report a dead drummer. In the van behind Eerie Taps."

"I see. Is there a reason you didn't call the emergency number?" Courtney scolding me, even subtly, meant she probably wasn't having a good day.

I felt my cheeks flushing with embarrassment. "Mrs. Gerards is working the faerock orders, so the call would have been routed up through dispatch at Port Rowan. With Lorne off today, I just cut out the middleman."

"You're sure he's dead?" Courtney's tone softened a little. Good. I hope she wasn't really mad at me.

Zoey stepped up next to me and gasped. I glanced inside the van. "Yep. That's a dead drummer."

"I'll call EMS to confirm and head that way myself. Alley behind Eerie Taps?"

"Yes," I said, only to have the call click off. Poor Courtney.

She didn't sound like she was having a good morning dealing with her old roommate.

Zoey had gone white and was leaning back against the building. I pulled her sideways, so she wasn't staring into the open door.

Randy had his own phone in hand, or so I assumed, since he had a large, hairy hand pressed up to his ear. "Suki? It happened again. Someone killed our new drummer... Right.... In the van. Okay." He dropped his hand. "She'll be right down."

The high-pitched whine of pixie wings sounded, and Willard flew into the van's open door, zipped around, and paused next to Geoff's body. I could just barely see his wings flash in the light leaking through the windshield. The front seats hid the drummer from our sight, but I imagined him pressing a tiny hand on Geoff's neck, checking for a pulse.

Willard zipped out and popped tall. Of course, he had a chocolate-covered doughnut—with sprinkles—in hand. His other hand held his phone, the camera pointed at the inside of the van. The fake click of a camera shutter sounded, and Willard's thumb flew over the screen. I assumed he was texting the image of the scene to Courtney.

"Strangled with what appears to be a guitar string. One of the thick ones," Willard said, taking a bite of the doughnut. "Was he a guitarist?"

"Drummer," Randy said. "Our third one this year."

"Were the other two murdered?" Willard asked, using his doughnut to point into the van.

"No. One was trampled by an elephant. The other got assaulted in Toronto. A woman's husband thought they were having an affair and caught him in the alley behind the bar we were playing at."

"Ouch." Willard flinched. "He survive the assault?"

"That one, yes. Only a few bruises. But it was the woman's neighbour he was having an affair with. Once the other husband found out, both gents came back and found him. Broke every one of his fingers."

More pixie wings sounded, and Suki popped tall between Randy and Willard. She stared into the van for a few seconds, then turned away, her face devoid of colour, and a hand pressed to her mouth.

"Maybe we should just get a drum machine and call it good," Suki said, shaking her head. "Our band is cursed against drummers."

7

W illard waved his half-eaten doughnut toward the van. "Wasn't there a movie where the band's drummers kept dying off?"

"Yeah. *This is Spinal Tap*," Randy said. "We've got a ways to go before we hit their record for drummer turn-over. Their count was eighteen if I remember correctly."

Willard checked his phone, then dropped it back in one of the many pockets on his medic flight suit. His normal role as the EMS in the town meant those pockets were filled with all sorts of medical and first aid stuff. Though, with Geoff's colour, it was obvious none of the medical stuff would do any good.

"Gonna need you all to stay here, but away from the crime scene," Willard added in a friendly tone. "Courtney will be here in a minute or two and begin the investigation. She'll need to speak to all of you."

A low, alert chime sounded in the air. It was magical, and one only fae could hear. Randy's disguise spell kicked in, and his appearance shifted to his tall, dusty-brown-haired human form. Which was good, as I spied DeAnn walking down the alley.

"Sammi!" She waved, approaching us.

"Hi DeAnn. Get your words in for the day?" I called out, then whispered to Randy. "Mundane coming."

"I noticed," he said and tapped the van door. Inside, the magical interior shifted, and the van appeared mundane again.

"Yep. All five thousand!" she said as she came up near the van. "Just in time for an early lunch. I was in the mood for shepherd's pie, wanna join–"

Her sentence cut off as she spied the drummer through the open doors of the van. "Ooooo! Another mystery. And I see you're on the case, Sammi."

"On the case?" I shook my head. "That's Courtney's job."

She stepped back from the van and started searching in the small backpack she carried as a purse. "But you solved the last murder so well. Ah. I've got my notebook right here. What are we going to title this one? The Case of the Deceased Drummer?"

"You're not going to write this up for the news are you?" Suki asked, leaning back against the side of the pub.

"She's a mystery writer. Our local *author...*" I put extra emphasis on the last word, in a way I hoped they recognized as a stand-in for calling her our local mundane.

"D. D. Zarius is my pen name." DeAnn held out a hand. "DeAnn Powers is my real name. So happy to meet you."

"Thanks. Suki Yoshino, and our bassist Randy Mueller," Suki said, taking her hand.

DeAnn forced a pleasant smile, trying not to look at the van where the dead drummer was. "Seriously. I loved the show. We all did. Especially the way you recovered after your guitarist broke all of his strings. I've never seen that happen. One or two at a time, but not all six at once. I hope he gets through tonight's show without a mishap."

Suki nodded slowly. "Marius is very energetic, and his strings were rather old. So glad you enjoyed the show."

A decent save by Suki. How does one explain to a mundane that a vamp with undead strength could easily break all the guitar strings every night if he's not careful?

Suki glanced back at the van. Fortunately, the open door shielded us from a view of the inside. "I'm not sure what we'll do about tonight. We're short a drummer."

Randy pointed toward the bar. "Told you I got drum patterns programmed in your keyboard."

"Basic patterns only, right? We still need to get that fine-tuned for each song." Suki rolled her lower lip in. "We'll have to skip the surf-rock closing set, though. There are too many drum solos in those."

"I've got the basic surf-beat programmed." Randy stroked his chin. "Marius might be able to substitute a guitar solo for one or two of the drum pieces."

Suki shook her head. "He's good, but surf-rock needs drums."

"So glad you're able to go on," DeAnn said, but took a little step back, eyeing each of the band members. "Where's your guitarist?"

"He's uh..." Randy volunteered, then paused, probably remembering DeAnn was the reason for his disguise spell.

"A late sleeper," Suki added.

Tires crunched in the gravel at the end of the alley. Court-ney, in the newly lettered Eerie Falls - Ontario Provincial Police vehicle, pulled up to block access. But it was Niki, getting out of the passenger side door that made me raise an eyebrow.

Courtney paused at the back hatch to the SUV and removed the evidence kit, a bag full of bags, gloves, a camera, and other stuff she might need at a murder scene. Niki, however, didn't pause. She headed right towards us.

"So, who found the dead guy?" Niki asked, not even bothering to introduce herself.

"Pardon Miss Durand, folks," Courtney said, stepping up next to the visiting politico. "Willard, take everyone inside the pub. Coroner is on the way, so I need to photograph the site and collect any evidence before they arrive."

Niki Durand looked around, then bent down and pulled a large tablet out of the evidence bag. She flipped it open and held the stylus ready to write. "Where's the stiff? Who found him?"

"OPP use only, Mizz Durand." Courtney grabbed the tablet from her.

Niki rolled her eyes, and I expected a teenager style *whatevs!* from her. But she just smiled and looked at the medic.

"And the stiff? Where is he?"

"The deceased," Willard said stiffly, "is in the van."

Niki leaned forward and peered in through the open side door. She shut her eyes, stepped back, and took a deep breath. Courtney just had time to jerk the evidence kit out from behind Niki's backpedal so the woman didn't trip over it. Court's glare at her old roomie went unnoticed.

My girlfriend shifted her eyes towards Willard. "Inside, please, everyone."

"I'll get the door unlocked." Zoey, grabbed the bar's bag of faerock and pulled a set of keys, which was actually her wand with a disguise spell active, out of her sleeve and headed toward the alley door to the bar.

"All right everyone. You heard the constable. Inside, please." Willard pointed toward the door with the last bit of his doughnut held between finger and thumb.

"Hang tight, folks," Willard said once we were in. "I'll go set up the police tape around the alley for Constable Courtney. Back in a jiffy."

He stayed tall, probably only until the door shut behind us. After that, he probably popped pixie to fly with the yellow police tape unrolling behind him. Willard would be back in a moment or two, as fast as he flew.

Inside the bar, Zoey already had several tumblers set up on the bar, lids off. She had the special dispenser thingie with the hose to the pop tanks in hand. I never knew what to call it. The contraption with a nozzle and push buttons on the back. Push one to get cola, push another to get lemon-lime. Zoey squirted a different type of pop into each glass. "I think I remembered everyone's beverage of choice from last night. No booze, for obvious reasons." She pushed the lidded drink tumblers forward. "Diet for Sammi and our author. Straight Coke for Randy, and Coke no bubbles for Suki."

"No bubbles?" DeAnn shook her head. "Why don't you want carbonation in your soda?"

Suki gave a weak smile. "They make me burp. Really bad." Since DeAnn had no idea that pixies existed, she wouldn't understand that pixies always took their sodas flat. Burping while flying could send a pixie way off course, usually in a backwards direction.

DeAnn and I took seats at a table in the middle of the room. Suki headed up on stage and turned on her keyboard and the tablet that was connected to it. Randy joined her after doffing his jacket. The T-shirt he wore was one cele-brating the fiftieth anniversary of Pink Floyd's album, *Dark Side of the Moon*. The one where the prism with the rainbow light was surrounded by a circular rainbow.

"I'll have a Cosmo with sweetened cranberry juice. Add a shot of grenadine too," Niki said from the hallway as she strode in from the alley.

Oh joy, I thought. We get to deal with her. But that meant Courtney got a reprieve. If it helped my girlfriend have some peace, I could put up with Niki for a short while.

Zoey rolled her lower lip in as Niki headed our way. I could see her calculating whether to give Niki what she demanded. She decided to play it safe and started mixing the cocktail.

"Sweet Cherry Cosmo, coming right up," Zoey said but rolled her eyes once Niki had passed the bar.

"Miss Cupertino, Miss Powers," Niki said and slid into a chair. "I hope I'm not imposing this time." She emphasized the *this time,* telling us she remembered our snub the night before.

"Not at all," DeAnn said with a polite smile and friendly tone. "What can we help you with, special assistant?"

"I just wanted to get an idea of what happened? Who found the body of that poor fellow?" Her smile was wide and well-practised. She was definitely on track to be a politician.

DeAnn turned to me.

I shrugged. "Zoey and I came back and found Randy in the alley, smoking and doing the crossword from the Fort Erie times. He went to open the van door, and all three of us saw at the same time."

"So, he, um..." Niki glanced back over her shoulder toward the stage, where Randy and Suki were testing out some of the drum patterns on Suki's keyboard. With their volume low, we could easily hold a conversation over the sound.

"He what?" DeAnn's tone was innocent, but I'd learned that she had a sharp wit and good detection skills about people. She wasn't fooled by Niki's friendly attitude.

"That hairy ape didn't have anything suspicious about him? He really seemed surprised the other fellow was dead?" Niki's eyes dropped, probably suspicious of the bassist.

I shrugged. "Nothing suspicious about him."

"Do you think the bassist killed the drummer?" DeAnn asked, picking up her pen and holding it to her pad.

Zoey set a tumbler in front in front of Niki.

"What is this?" Niki pointed at the lidded, wide bottom tumbler. "Cosmos don't go in metal cups. Especially with a lid."

"House rules," Zoey said politely, a smile growing on her face. "You sit with Sammi, you get either a to-go cup or a travel tumbler."

"Sit with Sammi?" Niki turned back to me, her anger turning to puzzlement.

I nodded. "I've been *cursed* with clumsiness." The emphasis on cursed caused Niki to raise an eyebrow.

DeAnn nodded. "She's right. I feel for Sammi. It's better to have that cup than to wear your drink out of here. I swear, she really is cursed, if you believe in that type of thing."

Zoey took the opportunity to head back to the bar and almost bumped into Willard. She stopped him and held out a hand in greeting. I assume she was introducing herself as a new pixie in town. Willard grinned and clapped her on the shoulder. His eyes started searching the room, though. He spied us and headed our way.

"Ladies. The constable wants me to take a few official

statements for the report." He looked at DeAnn first. "Miss Powers, if you please? Then Sammi. Courtney asked that I take your statement, for, um, obvious reasons."

"You mean because Sammi and Courtney are dating, and that would be a conflict of interests," DeAnn said, rising from her chair. "I don't have much to say, since I showed up after you did, officer."

"Still, we need to get an official statement," Willard said, keeping his tone official.

He led her to a booth well away from the rest of us and pulled a tablet from one of his pockets. DeAnn didn't notice that the pocket had seemed empty before the tablet appeared. The familiar magic static of a quiet spell activated around them. Fortunately, our author didn't even notice that.

"Why ever is a medic taking a police statement?" Niki shook her head.

"You know how small this town is?" I waved a hand toward the outside. "Willard is a reserve constable filling in whenever Lorne or Courtney is off duty, or when they have an emergency. There aren't many bobbies in the Ontario Provincial Police, and most of them are in the Toronto or Ottawa areas. So we get Willard instead of an orc."

Niki took the lid off her tumbler and sniffed, then tasted the content of the cup. "That's actually a good drink. Old Breezy doesn't make a bad Cosmo. I never knew Joey had it in him."

I dropped my chin and stared at Niki. The urge to uncap my drink and fling it in her face roared in, but I swallowed the idea. Instead, I laid my hands flat on the table, away from my cup.

"Her name is Zoey. Have some respect, will you!" I glared

at Niki but tried to keep still, so my curse wouldn't pick that moment to kick in. There was an uncapped cup on the table.

"Right, Zoey. I keep forgetting." Niki's smile slipped into the politician's grin again. Which didn't make me feel any better about her. Dead-naming and miss-gendering Zoey like that took Niki down a few more notches in my estimation. And she hadn't started very high on my list.

I wasn't sure what Niki wanted, but I felt that I should get the topic off of Zoey. "Did you know the deceased? I hear you were in university together…"

She shrugged. "A little from the Greek council. He was good with numbers. Drummers are like that, though. Guitarists are pretty good too. Excellent use of their hands. Did you ever date one?" Her smile slid into a coy, teasing smile, alluding to something.

I just raised an eyebrow, then gave a slow shake of my head, trying to keep as still as I could.

Niki leaned forward, both elbows on the table. Her fingers wrapped around her cup.

"Not into musicians? I wondered," Niki said, a sly smile on her face, "if you've ever had a chance to date a Zeta Iota Gamma? We make wonderful girlfriends." She dropped a hand and slowly wrapped her fingers around mine.

Behind her, the alley door opened and Courtney walked in. Her eyes locked on mine.

I jerked my hand back out of Niki's grip, my cheeks flushing in embarrassment. Courtney's stare made me shift in my seat, and my foot banged the table leg hard.

$$\maltese \quad 8 \quad \maltese$$

"**S**o..." Gord said two hours later, when I was back in the bookshop. He'd finished for the day and stopped in to hang out and get the scoop on the police action at Eerie Taps. We sat in the easy chairs in the centre section of the store. He was using a couple of pencils from the cup on the counter to tap out some drumbeats on his small table between the chairs. "You purposely let your klutz curse fly with that Niki woman?"

"Purposely, no. But Courtney was starting to snarl, and that made me very uncomfortable."

"And that woman ended up wearing her drink! Good use of the klutz curse."

My cheeks reddened at that. I shrugged, but Gord's grin was contagious, and my smile grew. "Yeah. I hadn't planned it that way. But I'll count this one as a win. Except..."

"What? Courtney didn't really think you were holding hands with that witch, did she?"

I opened my mouth but only shrugged, not sure what to say. "We, uh... didn't get a chance to talk about it. Courtney had come in because the coroner had taken charge of the scene. While that happened, she needed to get witness statements from Randy and Suki. She's still there waiting on Marius to wake up and getting statements from Darcy and anyone else who might have stayed after the show."

"What happened to Niki? I mean, after she splashed her drink into her face?"

That made my cheeks flare red again. I hated when my curse caused other people's discomfort. Gord knew me well enough to figure out what I was feeling.

"Oh, come on, Sammi. You know Niki deserved it."

I slowly nodded. "She did and not just for trying to wedge between me and Courtney." I paused a moment, debating with myself. "She also purposely dead-named and misgendered Zoey."

Gord's jaw dropped, and he stopped his pencil-drumming. "Rude! Yeah, she deserved a face full of booze. Did Zoey hear her insults?"

I shrugged. "No clue. But I suspect she might have. Zoey saw the splash and wasn't her normal quick self, bringing a clean rag over. You know pixies and their love of the no-spill-spell to suck up mistakes. Zoey was definitely moving at orc speeds, not pixie velocity."

A chuckle echoed from Gord. "Good for Zoey and for you for sticking up for her."

I sighed and looked out the front window. Courtney was still over at the bar.

"You've got that serious look. What are you thinking?"

Another shrug, but I turned back to Gord. "I really want

to, no, I need to talk with Courtney and make sure she knew that was all Niki's action and none of mine. There is no way I'd dump Court. Especially not for someone like that Niki. What was her sorority? Zeta Iota... something?"

"Figures," Gord said with more than a hint of derision. "She's a ZIG girl. There are some awesome people in the Greek orgs on campus. But at that school, I had more problems with ZIG girls. They were always stuck up and wanted you to know they were better than everyone."

"Maybe they're nicer at other colleges?" I shrugged, not having spent much, if any, time around sorority girls. Unless they came into the library, and then I helped them find their research materials, not talk about Greek life.

Gord chuckled. "Yeah. Neither of us was into Greek life. The PIXI girls were much friendlier."

"I forgot about the psi iota chi iota girls. With a name like that, you know it was all pixies."

"Yep. Since they had their own house, it was an unspoken rule across the houses that Pixies would only pledge PIXI."

"What about the other fae races? Did they have their own house like the pixies?"

"And I thought I was sheltered at college. You never got out much, did you?" Gord chuckled.

My cheeks warmed, getting redder, and I gave a shy shrug. "Why go out when all those books were in the library? The Greek guys could never actually get them back on the sorting carts. I was always cleaning up their research messes. Now, what about the other races? Did they have specialty houses?"

"The gnome girls and the lone dryad we had on campus didn't seem interested in pledging."

I nodded and glanced over toward Eerie Taps and spied a familiar shape crossing the street from Darcy's bar. Randy turned and walked our way. He pulled the door open and smiled when he saw me rise.

"Been meaning to stop in and see what you've got in here," Randy said. He still wore his Pink Floyd t-shirt, but he was back to his Sasquatch form.

"What do you like to read?" I asked, unsure what a tall and hairy bass player would like.

"Napoleonic history? Or English Civil war?" Randy let a smile break through the whiskers on his face. "What, you didn't expect me to be a history buff?"

I chuckled and led him over to the correct section. "A couple of memoirs here. Including the new one from Sir Nathan Trimbolt, as told to his brother, Edward, the current Lord Trimbolt." I pulled the book out of the stack. "My friend Ebrel sent me three copies that Lord Trimbolt himself signed. This is the Fae Edition. You get the full story, not the watered down one to hide any magical mentions."

"That name sounds familiar. Wasn't Nathan Trimbolt killed at the battle?" Randy took the tome from me and flipped to the half-title page at the front of the book. *Eddie Trimbolt,* was scrawled in green ink on the page.

"Not at the battle," I said, remembering what I'd read in the foreword. "He died in Wales a few months after the battle. My friend helped solve his murder and install the new Lord Trimbolt back in his family's lands."

"Ah, then it will be good to get the reports from Sir Nathan. Says on the cover he was a fae member of Lord Wellington's force." Randy flipped a few pages. In the background, Gord kept drumming with his pencils. I recognized the beat from one of the rock songs the band had played before.

Randy turned his head, listening. After a few seconds, he passed me the book. "I'll take it."

"Anything else?" I headed to the counter but paused to see if he responded. Instead of following me, the bassist was watching Gord.

"Be careful," I said with a chuckle. "Gord might have to run down to the high school and get his marching band bass drum to help you out."

"I was hoping he might." Randy chuckled. "Do you still play the skins?"

Gord nodded, his eyes getting wide. "When I need some quiet time."

That made me laugh. "Drums are not quiet."

"You know what I mean," Gord said.

Randy nodded and walked to the counter where he tapped his wand to pay for the book. "He's right. Musicians love to dive into a piece or two and lose ourselves in the music. It quiets the mind like meditation."

He turned back toward Gord. "We've got a drum kit, but no drummer. Do you mind coming over to the bar right now and showing us what you've got?"

Gord's jaw dropped open. "Seriously? You want me to audition?"

"A temporary gig only. You know the surf-beat?"

Gord started tapping out a beat like boom, chi chi, boom chi chi, boom chi chi, boom chi chi... or as close to that as he could using the wood of the pencil for the boom and the metal sleeve near the eraser for the chi chis.

"Come on over, man," Rand tilted his head toward the door. "Suki and Marius need to see what you've got."

"Love to!" Gord rose, returning the pencils to the cup.

"I'm off work tomorrow, so I can play tonight if you need me to."

"Suki is the boss," Randy said, pulling the door open. "We'll see if you can impress her."

"Good luck!" I waved at Gord, sharing his smile.

"Thanks, Sammi!"

An hour later, Gord was still in the bar, which was probably good for him and the band. I puttered around the shop, keeping up with online orders, and checking for estate sales, and other notices that might lead me to a trove of fae books. Even though Eerie Tomes was a general bookstore and made decent money from stocking trade paperbacks for the tourist season, our real specialty was in old magical tomes and books about fae and magic. For fae consumption only, of course.

Instead of sitting in my office, I stayed out front with my laptop at the counter. My eye kept wandering up to look out the front window. Courtney's EF-OOP vehicle was still parked, blocking the alley. The inspector from Fort Erie was here. His unmarked SUV still screamed COP car. Plain wheels, darker tinted windows. He and Courtney had been out in the alley a few times but mostly stayed inside.

I wanted to talk with her. No, I needed to talk with her. Explain that Niki was using me, and I hadn't planned any of that handholding. But, with a murder to investigate, Court needed to do her police thing. That was important. First, because we had a killer in town, again. Second, with Lorne on a day off, this was probably Court's case to handle. Well, to assist with now that Inspector Robert from Fort Erie was down here again. He'd take over the case. But I knew Court wanted to climb the ranks and get an inspector position someday. This case would help her record if she handled it correctly.

And that darn Niki had to try to insert herself in between us. Gah!

I took a deep breath and looked at my hand. I'd crunched up the top sheet of the pad I'd been making notes on. Fortunately, there weren't many notes. I smoothed it out and sighed. A chime sounded, and an internet order popped up for a standard fae text. I kept the price on it low so we could move copies and get into people's minds as a good source for books on magical subjects. Another glance out the window showed no new activity across the street.

With another sigh, I rose, fetched the book from the stacks, and headed to the office to wrap it for delivery. While I was in the back, I got a text from Gord.

I'm playing tonight! If I do well, Suki said I can play tomorrow as well!

Great! I text back and promised I'd be there tonight, then turned back to wrapping up the order.

I had just finished when the bell on the front door sounded, so I made my way out front. Cleo was crouched by the front counter, her tail twitching in a way that said she was waiting to pounce. That meant she still hadn't rid our shop of all mice.

The man who stood at the rack of westerns was familiar.

"Mr. Morosov. Another vacation in Eerie Falls?"

The man from the *Tisserand*, the Russian Wereshark Mafia run gambling boat that sailed Lake Erie, turned with a grin.

"Not this week, Miss Cupertino. Our boat is getting ready to sail. We open this weekend." He turned back and ran a finger along the stacks, then pulled a book out to add to the stack of six or so already piled on a nearby table. He then added another and another after that. "I will have less time to read, but also less time to visit. So I make special trip to get extra books."

"Thank you. You remember that you can trade in the books you've already read?" I'd previously explained the exchange program we ran in the shop. "We stock used books and give a credit for any you bring back."

"I remember. But I donate all the books to the ship's library. Not everyone who boards like to gamble. Some of our guests just want good food and to enjoy the view of the lake."

He pulled several more books off the shelves and passed the stack to me. I was surprised to see a couple of DeAnn's books in the stack.

"Branching out into mysteries?"

"Why not?" Morosov shrugged but gave me a polite smile. "The author is local, right?"

"Yes, but very mundane." I tapped our stuffed owl on the counter. "She's the one setting off the detectors all across town."

"No magic in her books then?"

I nodded. "Very normal murder mysteries. No magic."

"Good. I get tired of magic always solving problems. That's why I read westerns. Character or a six shooter solves the problems."

I chuckled hearing a man with a Russian accent speak so fondly about American Westerns.

As I rang his order up, Gramps came in from the back office. He pulled a cup of coffee from the pot we kept behind the counter and nodded a greeting to our customer, then dropped into one of the reading chairs with the Fort Erie paper in his hands.

I passed the books back to the wereshark. "Thank you,

Mr. Morosov. And... I don't remember if I've asked. What is it you do on the *Tisserand*?"

"Assistant Director of Security," he said and gripped half a dozen of the paperbacks to drop them into his shopping bag. Even it was decorated with the grey and black logo of the gambling boat. Once he had the other half of the stack of books in his bag, he fished around in his jacket pocket and pulled out a stack of business cards. He thumbed through them and then passed me one outlined with a silver border.

My eyes grew wide, and I pushed the card back to him. "You gave me the wrong card. This is a voucher for a suite on the ship."

"Not wrong. Is a gift." Morosov smiled, waving off my attempt to give it back to him. "Good for up to five days. You have all of this season to use it. You bring your girlfriend. Have nice getaway on our boat. You and she both need to relax."

"Marvellous idea, Sammi," Gramps said and nodded toward Eerie Taps where Courtney's police SUV still sat. "Sounds as though she'll need some time away after this new mess."

"Here, let me key it to you." Morosov pulled his wand from his sleeve and tapped the card as I held it. "Now it only good for you. No giving it away."

"A princely gift." Gramps grinned and nodded. "I looked into getting a suite on board to take Betty. It was beyond my budget. Say thank you, Sammi."

I swallowed my inclination to argue. "Thank you. I don't know when Courtney can get time off."

Morosov looked out the window, then turned back, jerking a thumb over his shoulder at the bar. "Looks like inspector from the detachment at Fort Erie is here again. You going to solve another murder?"

"Me?" I shook my head. "That's Courtney's job."

"Well, once you and she catch the bad guy, you come see our boat." Morosov grinned, showing his white teeth. Which always sent a chill up my spine when I knew I was dealing with a shifter. "We treat you nice, and let you both relax."

A s he left the bookshop, Morosov held the door open for DeAnn.

She wore a devious smile as she entered. "Well. You won't believe who I saw hanging out around the alley at Taps."

I raised an eyebrow but let a grin escape. "You sound just like Mrs. Needles."

"Exactly! Her!" DeAnn's head bounced with enthusiasm. "I just haven't been able to figure out how that old busybody would know the drummer. Nor why she'd want to murder him."

"Wait! You saw Mrs. Needles in the alley where the murder happened and think she killed Geoff the drummer?"

Cleo's mental chuckle echoed in my mind. *I wouldn't put murder outside of her reach. But that old witch would far rather kill with words than with deeds.*

I let my eyes focus past DeAnn where Cleo lay atop the

back of an easy chair opposite where Gramps sat reading his paper. But DeAnn's voice brought my gaze back to her.

"It's always the person you least expect." DeAnn wandered over to the shelf where I had a few of her books front facing on small stands. "Here in *The Notorious Knitter of Death* I had the town gossip misdirect everyone with all of her talk and sharing of half-truth secrets. She was really the killer."

"Your town busybody ran a knitting shop?" I shook my head. "That's a bit too much of a real life meets fiction coincidence."

"No, the sleuth ran the yarn shop. Yarn shops, tea shops, bookshops are all popular professions for amateur sleuths." She replaced the book, then turned and crossed her arms, staring at me.

"Sooooo..." I let the syllable hang for a moment. "You think Mrs. Needles..."

"She's definitely on the suspect list. When I wrote my story, I didn't realize the killer was Roberta right away. She stole knitting needles from two rivals and killed off the man who had broken her heart back in high school. She'd had her knickers in a twist for almost thirty years before she stabbed him. Now we need to track down how that old busybody knows the drummer."

I shook my head, trying to clear it and get her stories straight. "You think your Roberta was dating Geoff in high school? I'm confused."

DeAnn tilted her head in a quizzical look at me.

"Never mind," I said.

"I miss my long chats with Leonard... That would be Mr. Needles," Gramps explained to DeAnn and stood. "He died a few years before Patty passed. I bored Sammi incessantly trying to hold conversations with her after losing my two favourite conversation partners."

"You weren't that bad," I said, trying to keep Gramps from reliving some of the emotions we both dealt with when Grams passed.

Oh, he bored the socks off you and anyone he could corner, dear. Cleo raised her head and started licking her paw. *I only pretended to listen to half of what he yammered on about.*

That made me smile. I, too, had learned the subtle art of listening just enough to know when to respond to one of Gramps's soliloquies and tune out the rest of what he lectured on.

Gramps leaned back in a stretch. "I told Betty I'd be ready for dinner before the concert tonight. And it looks like they've finally got the tavern open. Can you close the shop tonight, Sammi?"

That was a question I could answer. "Sure thing, Gramps. I want to come to the show, too, since Gord is playing."

"Excellent. Betty and I will save you a seat. Will Courtney be with you?"

I shrugged. She and Inspector Robert were still inside the bar. "I don't even know if she's still talking to me."

DeAnn "Oh dear. Have you not talked with her since that awful Niki grabbed your hand?"

"Trouble in paradise?" Gramps paused on his way to the office, giving me a look of concern.

"Uh... That Niki woman from the MPP's office tried to insert herself in between Court and I, right as Courtney walked in. But Court was all official with the investigation and only glared at us. No time for us to talk about it."

DeAnn laughed. "Sammi conveniently kicked a table leg and made that evil woman spill her drink all over herself."

My cheeks warmed as Gramps chuckled. "Well, I know better than to get in the middle of that. Let me know if you need my help watching the shop while you sort that out, Sammi."

I sighed but gave him a thin smile. "Thanks Gramps. We'll work it out. If Courtney weren't neck deep in a murder investigation, I would have taken care of it right then. But by the time I could get away from Niki, Courtney was already interviewing another witness. Or suspect. Or whatever she considers them."

"We'll save you a couple of seats, just in case," Gramps said and headed back to the office. A moment later, I heard him exit through the back door.

"Text her," DeAnn said.

"What?"

She pointed at my phone on the counter. "Text Courtney. See if she's doing dinner. That way, you two can talk and square things up."

"Yeah. I probably should." I typed out a quick text to see if she was going to be free for dinner. After a tense moment of waiting, I let my breath out.

Can't.

Gotta go to Ft. Eerie for the preliminary victim exam.

Willard is on duty tonight.

I showed the text to DeAnn.

"Well, at least she's talking. Even if it's just short texts."

I nodded. "That's how she always is. Not too wordy. Direct and to the point. But I can't get a read on whether she's miffed about it. And if she's going to Fort Erie for the autopsy or whatever..." I let my thought trail off. Court liked Gord and would want to see him with the band if she knew he was getting a to play with them.

"I'm surprised she's the one going," DeAnn said, turning to watch out the windows. "Shouldn't Lorne be handling that?"

Courtney, Niki, and a rugged, human appearing Inspector Robert were heading to the two dark SUVs at the curb. Niki, of course, had to slide into the passenger side of Courtney's EF-OPP vehicle. I felt sorry for Court. She'd had to deal with Niki all day and now, all evening too.

I shook my head. "Lorne is off on an extended fishing weekend."

"Ooo! So it's Courtney's time to shine." DeAnn flashed a smile, which faded quickly. "Oh dear, I shouldn't be happy when someone's been murdered. But seeing a friend like Courtney have a chance to prove herself... that's good, right?"

"Yeah. Courtney took the post here to get out of the big city danger zones." And this is a fae town, which I couldn't really explain to DeAnn. "She's trying to work her way up to an inspector position. This is just what she needs on her CV. Or whatever cops have."

"I'm sure she'll get there in no time." DeAnn glanced at her watch, then rubbed her belly. "How long until you close up? I'm getting hungry, and Brigitte's grills smelled sooo good when I was walking over."

I glanced at the clock over the door. "Give me half an hour, and I'll call it close enough. I can't wait until summer hits and Brigitte opens up all week long."

DeAnn and I walked down the half-block to get to C&B BBQ. The wooden sign over the door looked like someone had stamped a giant branding iron on it with the letters in the name. Under the logo, *Texas style BBQ Ribs, Brisket, Pork, and Chicken* were also burned into the wood. The C was for Carlos, and the B for our friend Brigitte. The couple had been married when Carlos was murdered right outside the place a few months before.

DeAnn pulled the door open for me, and the neon lights behind the counter gleamed with the same logo as above the door. The large, glowing C&B flickered and turned from Red to Blue as DeAnn entered the shop. That was Brigitte's mundane detector spell kicking in.

The French-Canadian pixie was working the counter herself today. Behind her, a window cut into the wall, framed her male kitchen help. One of the local younger pixie adults.

Brigitte's red hair almost gleamed with pixie highlights that shimmered with pixie inherent magic. "Mademoiselles! Welcome again!"

"Oh, always a warm welcome here. I love it," DeAnn said, stepping up to the counter.

"Oui. I am a warm person." Brigitte looked at me. I repressed my smile, knowing her nature as a flame pixie. DeAnn had her memory blanked of the one time she saw Brigitte in her tiny form. But Brigitte and I remembered how she helped catch the killer.

"You've done well with the place," DeAnn said, looking around at the decor.

"Mercí. It is not the restaurant Carlos wanted, but it is the one I'm best at running."

DeAnn chuckled. "I never knew Texas-style barbecue was a French-Canadian specialty?"

"Let us say that I am at home on the grill." Brigitte shared a grin with me. Both of us knew her fiery nature and could share the chuckle.

"I'm sure that anyone Jonathan teaches to grill is well trained."

"Oh, oui! Colonel Jonathan and his wife are good friends.

Everything on our menu is his recipe." Behind us, the bell on the door jingled with someone else coming in.

"We'd better order," I nudged DeAnn.

"Of course. I'll start with a smoked sausage sandwich, extra onions, and the mac-n-cheese."

"Brisket, and the Mac-n-cheese," I said.

"I'm paying," DeAnn said, pulling her debit card out. "My newest release is doing well, so this is my celebration meal!"

"Well, I suppose I should read one of your trite little whodunnits then," Mrs. Needles said from behind us. "And I don't want to be seeing Lenora Needles anywhere inside the pages."

"Oh," DeAnn rolled her lower lip in before turning towards the town gossip. "I told you yesterday, I always change names to protect the guilty. You won't have to worry about that."

She and Mrs. Needles stared at each other for a long moment. I shifted my weight, unsure if they were going to come to blows right then and there.

"How's your son, Lenora?" I volunteered the question trying to defuse the animosity that was growing between the two women.

"Oh, Robert is in town. He came in last evening while that awful band was blaring whatever poor excuse for music they claimed to play."

"Oh," I said, tightening my lips. "Courtney and I actually enjoyed it."

"You youngsters would. It's not the type I enjoy. And they should really turn down the volume. Don't those gizmos, what do you call them, amplifiers? Don't they have volume knobs?"

"They do," I said.

"And they go all the way up to eleven," DeAnn added, her

devious smile growing. "While we're there tonight, I'll suggest they turn it up so you can hear better."

Mrs. Needles glared at her.

"You said Robert's in town?" I asked, trying to distract Lenora from DeAnn.

"Yes. He was coming in to meet a friend from college." The gossip shrugged. "But that's moot now."

"College, eh?" I raised an eyebrow.

"Your son was going to meet the dead drummer!" DeAnn's eyes went wide. "That's why you were snooping around the alley. You think he might have killed that poor drummer."

"What? No! How dare you accuse my Robert of that!"

DeAnn laughed and crossed her arms. "I didn't accuse him. I accused *you* of thinking that he did."

Lenora Needles's hand darted into the oversized shoulder bag she always carried. She jerked out two blue metal knitting needles and stopped with them almost under DeAnn's chin. "You take that back!"

DeAnn chuckled. "See. Motive to kill, right there. Making threats. I told you she might be the prime suspect."

"Sammi! Your order is ready," Brigitte called from behind us. I heard the catch of worry in her tone.

Grateful for the interruption, I pulled DeAnn by the arm to turn around. "Would you carry the tray? You know how I am."

The bell on the door jingled, and in walked Willard, this time in an OPP uniform.

"Going to knit our local author a new sweater?" He eyed the knitting needles.

Mrs. Needles slowly lowered her makeshift weapon.

"I had better not see any of this in your books." She jammed the needles back into her bag, stabbing the skein of red yarn peeking out of the wide opening. "And I will purchase them to make sure."

"Excellent," DeAnn chuckled. "I've made another lifelong reader. Let me know if you'd like the books autographed. Always happy to help a faithful reader."

❧ 10 ❧

I grabbed a table by the gas fireplace in the centre of the room. DeAnn stopped at the drink fountain and filled our to-go cups with pop.

"I'm glad Brigitte decided to make this place counter service," DeAnn said, sliding the tray on the table between us. "Eerie Falls isn't a place that needs a three-star restaurant with fancy tablecloths."

Willard stopped by our table, his own order in a to-go sack, and looked at DeAnn.

"Do I need to speak to Lenora about brandishing weapons in public?"

I glanced at my author friend wondering what she'd say.

She smiled and shook her head. "No. Just a polite misunderstanding. But that woman is definitely on the suspect list. Did you see how fast she drew those weapons."

"Suspect?" Willard shook his head. "Don't you two go getting involved in this mess. I remember last time. Town hall on fire, you two held at gunpoint. Let Courtney and the Inspector handle this."

DeAnn looked up at Willard. "You didn't mention yourself in that list. Don't you want in on cornering the murderer and bringing that crazy old bat to justice?" She ended with a sly chuckle.

"Unfortunately, no. I've got politician duty." He raised his sack. "I'll eat this on my rounds. Miss Durand should be back from Timmie's soon. I'm supposed to meet her at Town Hall and answer any questions she has."

I rolled my eyes, but DeAnn asked what I was thinking. "She didn't try to go with Courtney and the Inspector?"

Willard chuckled and shook his head. "She didn't look too pleased when the Inspector ordered her to stay in Eerie Falls. He threatened to call her MPP and declare she was interfering with the investigation."

"So you get to chaperone Niki Durand?" DeAnn gave him a comforting look. "Sorry. She's honked off almost everyone she meets here."

"See if you can figure out what she's doing here," I suggested. "Something about her makes me think she's here on a vendetta to screw with Courtney's career."

Willard raised an eyebrow but didn't say anything, giving me a silent invitation to continue.

"They were roommates in college for a brief time. I was getting strong jealousy vibes off Niki earlier today."

DeAnn nodded in agreement. "And she tried to steal Courtney's girlfriend. Grabbing her hand this morning."

"Is that what prompted that commotion at Taps?" Willard asked. "I was busy taking notes and heard a thud and Miss Durand cry out in surprise."

I nodded but shrugged. "Courtney's timing was terrible,

walking in right as Niki propositioned me and grabbed my hand."

"So you threw her drink into her face?"

"No." I felt my cheeks flushing. Embarrassment gave way to anger. "But I should have. She had to have planned that. How did she know Court was coming into the bar right then?"

"Magic?" DeAnn asked.

I shot her a glare, thinking we'd given something away about being fae. She just grinned and gave a little chuckle.

"Niki is definitely someone I'd peg as a witch if magic really existed." DeAnn shook her head. "Probably just weird timing and a coincidence."

"We'll go with that," I said, and looked back to Willard. "Good luck on babysitting duty tonight."

"Oh, I'll bore her to tears, driving around the town every few hours and sitting at town hall in between rounds until the evening shift ends. Good thing I picked up extra doughnut holes to get through the shift today."

He gave a jaunty salute and headed for the exit.

After DeAnn and I finished our meal, we headed over to Taps. Gramps and Betty had a booth near the stage. The place was fairly full already, and we still had an hour until the band was supposed to begin the first set.

Once we sat, Gramps pointed to the bar where all the stools were occupied. Darcy was behind the bar with Zoey and another pixie server running back and forth with trays full of drinks and dishes.

"And...?"

"Figured you'd recognize Bob Needles. He stopped by our booth when we wandered in."

I shook my head but peered at the patron. "Oh. Third stool from the left. Was he here last evening?"

"Got in late, from what he said." Gramps chuckled. "Seems his mother kept trying to get him to move back home with her."

I turned back to the table. If Bob Needles was in town for the weekend, we'd have plenty of time to catch up later.

"That old busybody only cares about getting gossip." Betty shook her head. I noticed she had her arm tucked in through Gramps's elbow.

"Mrs. Needles stopped by yesterday to inquire about you two." I giggled and elbowed DeAnn. "Our local author threatened to put her in a book."

"As the victim or the killer?" Betty gave a devious grin. "Too bad she couldn't be both."

"Hmmmm...." DeAnn pursed her lips. "I wonder if I could make that work somehow?"

"Other authors have done it, so why not?" I grinned.

"Sammi! Long time, eh?"

I looked up to find Bob Needles smiling at me.

"Hi Bob! This is DeAnn, our local *author* from the States."

"Ah, pleased to meet you," he said as DeAnn leaned around me to shake his hand. "Mother has mentioned you."

"Probably not nicely," DeAnn said with a chuckle that sounded half-way like a snort of disbelief.

"Well, this is mother we're talking about." His cheeks went red.

I tapped DeAnn to scoot over, and I slid to make room for Bob. The tables near us were all occupied, so he wasn't able to swing a chair around to sit at the end of our table. The booth was big enough that we could fit but barely.

"Your mom said something about you coming down to watch the band?"

"Yeah, I knew Geoff from college. We were in business school together. I got to be his mentor early on, since I was three years ahead of him. He took over as treasurer of the student body council when I graduated."

"I'm sure you've heard what happened to him?"

"With a mother like mine, of course I heard." Bob rolled his eyes up to stare at the ceiling. "Poor fellow. He'd emailed me, knowing I was from Eerie Falls. Said he got a gig playing here for a few nights. It wasn't a far drive, so I came down to get in touch with him. Funny how we were both in Toronto this past decade and never found the time to chat."

DeAnn had leaned forward, listening. "Did you get a chance to talk with him? I mean, before...?" She waved a hand to indicate the murder without directly naming the act.

"Yeah. I stayed last night long enough to have a drink with him. We chatted for a while. I got to meet the other band members, but they didn't seem to trust him much. He was a definite outsider."

"Yeah..." I shrugged. Bob and I were friends, but not as close as me and Gord. Still, I felt like I should give him the rundown on Geoff's own actions. "Your friend is a groper. Got slapped by the lead singer and tried to feel up Zoey too."

Bob just nodded. "I'm surprised he's not in jail then. Geoff always had wandering hands. His fraternity brothers had to lean heavily on him to stop. That didn't help much when they weren't around. He never learns."

"That kind never does," Betty said.

"Yeah... Geoff ended up with some broken bones and several instances of black eyes." Bob pursed his lips. "He made the mistake of getting frisky with the girlfriend of the star of the hockey team. Some of the team found him walking back alone from an evening class. He wasn't grabby for the rest of the year."

"Why don't people like him learn? Ugh!" I blew out a breath that was half anger and half sigh.

Bob shrugged. "How about you? Mom said you'd found someone. Getting serious yet?"

I grinned, then shrugged. "We're getting close to serious. I'd introduce you tonight, but Courtney is up in Fort Erie with the Inspector."

Bob raised an eyebrow. "You look worried. Because she's a cop? I'm not on any wanted posters, am I?"

I sucked in a breath, not wanting to keep sharing my concerns.

But DeAnn leaned forward again. "Sammi got accosted by that Niki girl earlier today. Right as Courtney walked into the bar, Niki grabbed Sammi's hand."

"Niki Durand? I heard she was in the area. Thought she'd have headed back to Ottawa by now?"

"Why does everyone know her except me?" I shook my head.

"Because you were a few years after us in college," Bob said and chuckled. "And I bet you spent most of your time in the library, never played sports, and didn't go Greek?"

He had a point. I didn't have many friends from college since I had spent most of my time in the book stacks.

"Well, I like to read..." My cheeks were warming, so I tried shifting topics. "How about you? Any significant others?"

Bob shrugged. "Nothing special. A few girlfriends from time to time. We just never seem to want to get serious for very long."

Behind him, Randy, looking like a tall human with long

hair, came out to the stage and started powering on the equipment. He stepped up to the mic Suki used. "Check! Check! Pay your tabs!"

Bob turned to watch, then looked back at me. "Figured they'd take a breather since Geoff died?"

"Gord is playing drums for them."

Bob's puzzled look shifted into a grin. "Good for him. Figured Gord was too shy, like you, to ever hit a stage."

"Check... Check... Credit Card..." Randy's voice rumbled again. He went through all of the various mics and checked each. Suki, then Marius, came up to the stage. Just about everyone in the place let out a holler, a whoop, or a whistle a moment later when Gord came out. His cheeks flushed red, but he raised his sticks in a friendly wave.

"Let me go reclaim my seat at the bar," Bob said, rising. "Darcy is giving me the evil eye for taking too long."

Suki tapped a few keys on the keyboard, while Marius and Randy ran their own checks on the guitar and bass. All of them, including Gord, wore an aloha shirt similar to their outfits from the night before. Gord had a few in his closet, so he must have run home to change before the show.

"Hellooooo Eerie Falls," Suki called into the mic. "We are Suki and the Sasquatches."

"Speak for yourself," Marius chimed in. "Only one of us has feet big enough to qualify."

"I dunno," Randy said, grinning behind his beard. "Let's check the new guy out. How big are your shoes, new guy?"

Gord, thoroughly embarrassed now, shrugged.

"Let's see em," Marius chided him.

"Shoes, Gord!" Suki said, and repeated it, motioning the crowd to take up the chant.

I burst out laughing as the crowd chanted along with her. "Shoes, Gord, shoes, Gord!"

Gord gave a big sigh and bent over from the stool behind the drum kit. He pulled off one of his Doc Martin sneakers and held it up. Randy grabbed it, slipped off one of his sandals, and held the two up. Randy's footwear was twice the size of Gord's shoe.

"Nope, sorry, kid. You and the long-haired hippy are only honorary Sasquatches." He passed the shoe back while the crowd laughed. Once Gord had his sneaker back on, Randy leaned into the mic. "Take us in, kid."

Gord set the beat by banging his sticks together, then launched into the first song. Early rock kept us going for several songs. Suki excelled on the keyboards with *Great Balls of Fire*. Marius got wound up with a couple songs from Elvis. Gord kept up with all of them.

As the first set wound down, I glanced at my watch. They'd been playing for over forty minutes already.

Suki turned sideways again as the applause slowed. "Should we give the new kid a break?"

"Naw," Randy said with a chuckle. "I say we make him star in the next set."

"Star? You don't mean..." She let it trail off, a knowing smirk on her face.

"I do mean..." Randy grinned. "Drum solo. Surf style."

Gord ran a short solo, moving from drum to drum, while running the underlying surf beat of *boom, chi chi, boom, chi chi...*

"The kid ain't half bad," Marius said when Gord slowed. "I say we let him carry us for the next set."

"Sounds like a plan," Randy added. "Give us fifteen minutes, folks. Got to get some refreshments."

Randy hit a button on the sound system and recorded

classic 60s rock songs played at a much quieter volume. Gord peeled himself out from behind the drums, grabbed a towel, and dabbed the sweat from his face. He headed our way.

"You were great!" I bounced out of the booth and clapped him on the arm but regretted it as my palm came back wet.

"Sorry." Gord grinned and held the towel towards me. He was a sweaty mess. But he'd been banging away on a drum kit for the last three-quarters of an hour.

"What's going on over there?" DeAnn had slid out of the booth and pointed at the stage.

Courtney and Inspector Robert stood at the side of the stage. Marius looking puzzled at something Courtney held. He nodded, then looked up.

Suki and Randy watched from the stage. Courtney pulled a card out of her pocket, and my belly flopped.

Inspector Robert slapped a metal bracelet around one of Marius's wrists, stepped behind him, and cuffed the other wrist.

Gord groaned. "Oh, no! There goes the rest of our show..."

11

"Sammi! You've got to help get Marius off the hook. He didn't kill Geoff." Gord sat looking at me. Suki and Randy each had pulled a chair up around one of the now empty tables in the pub. Once Marius had been led off, the concert was declared over, and the crowd returned to its normal Friday night buzz.

I shook my head. "Why me? And who else could have done it?"

"We wouldn't kill our own drummer," Suki said.

"Even Marius, he... ummm..." Randy glanced at DeAnn. "Marius is young, but he's not that out of control."

I knew what he meant. Newer vampires didn't always have control of their emotions. The lust for blood was strong in the younger ones.

Suki tapped my arm to draw my attention. "Gord said you solved the last murder here in town."

I felt my cheeks burn with embarrassment. "Well, yes... but I had a lot of help."

"No, it was all you," DeAnn said. She looked at Suki and held her hand out.

"Remember? She's the author. Mystery books. Between Sammi and DeAnn they should be able to figure this out," Gord said.

DeAnn shook her head. "I don't know what good I'll be. The last real mystery in town was all Sammi. I only handle the fictional ones."

Suki glanced between DeAnn and me, sharing a weak smile with each of us. "Well, we would really appreciate your help in finding the killer and getting Marius out of trouble."

"Look. I don't even know where to start." I shrugged, shaking my head. "Why'd they arrest him?"

"I barely caught sight of it," Randy said, jerking a big thumb over his shoulder towards the stage. "But they had one of his guitar picks in that plastic bag. The girl cop said Geoff was clutching it in his hand."

"Uh, oh. Not good." I shook my head. "Courtney and the inspector wouldn't act on flimsy evidence."

"Well, Marius didn't do it." Suki crossed her arms.

"How did one of his guitar picks end up in the dead guy's hand, then?" I glanced between them. No one had an answer.

Gord looked back at the stage and pointed. "Look at Marius's mic stand. He's got a pick holder attached to it."

He was correct. Half a dozen blood red picks were tucked into the plastic thingy attached to the metal pole. Randy rose and took a few steps towards the stage. He plucked one of the rounded triangles from the thingy and passed it to me.

It was a standard pick, thin but sturdy plastic with two rounded corners and one that was more pointed. Both sides were not only blood red, that rich crimson colour, but one side also had a logo. In black type, a large gothic M was embossed, but the lower legs ended with two curved white points, like vampire teeth.

DeAnn leaned in to get a look past my shoulder. "Oooooo! He's very goth, isn't he? He likes to role-play the vampire bit."

"Role-play, yeah, he's good," Suki interjected quickly.

I tapped my lips with a finger, thinking. "It would be easy to get one of his picks, wouldn't it?"

Randy nodded, then pointed back to the stage.

"Anyone could have grabbed one off the stand. And he drops them sometimes when he gets energetic. They slip out of his grasp. He likes to flirt and toss them to cute girls in the crowd."

"Hmmmm." DeAnn leaned back and crossed her arms. "Sammi and I didn't get a pick tossed to either of us."

"Were you flirting back with him?" Suki asked, her smile growing.

"Well, no. That's not why I'm here in Eerie Falls. I had enough with dating and with husbands. Time to be on my own without men for a while."

"Unlike Geoff," Randy said with a shake of his head, "Marius is very polite with those he'd like to, um... date."

I had never dated a vampire, though I had tried to get Darcy to notice me in that way. Evidently vamps get a lot of attention from those who want more than just a relationship or just a roll in the hay. Those folks really want to get their necks nibbled on by the undead for the thrill.

Suki nodded. "He's good about making sure he only engages with those that return his attentions."

DeAnn slid her lips sideways, like she did when she was thinking. "Oh... He only takes them back to his crypt, or whatever, if they want to go. Quite the gentleman then."

"He really is," Suki agreed.

DeAnn tapped a finger to her lips. "We know Marius took offence when Geoff grabbed you yesterday."

Suki sighed and nodded. "Marius is too much of a gentleman. Geoff was definitely not one. They clashed often in the week we've been together."

Randy drummed his large fingers on the table in a rolling wave. "Marius is protective of Suki. Geoff's reputation almost kept him out of the band. This was supposed to be a test run for him. He heard we were coming down here to Darcy's bar and really wanted in. I was going to program drum tracks into Suki's keyboard and get along without a drummer until he showed up."

"Why'd you let him into the band then?" I shook my head, trying to understand. "If he had a reputation like that, and you've got a female lead that he's going to go after?"

Suki blew out a breath. "I keep asking that too. But our last fill-in drummer got called in for a three-week recording session that paid better than we could promise, so we were getting desperate enough to bring Geoff along. Real drums are so much better than what I can add through the keyboard."

"Well, no wonder Courtney and that inspector fellow are suspecting Marius." I waved toward the stage. "Court was here with me for lunch yesterday when Marius sprang up and grabbed Geoff. She saw him act aggressively, even if Geoff deserved it. Then, they supposedly find one of the guitar picks clenched in the dead drummer's hand."

"But, in the van, Marius could have dropped a pick anywhere in there." Randy shook his head. "He and I jam often in the back while we're travelling. We all take turns driving. There are probably guitar picks all over the interior."

"Why would Geoff have one in his hand?" I shook my

head, trying to picture the murder. "Would Marius have handed him the pick as a distraction to wrap the guitar string around his neck? That would be silly."

"Wouldn't you have to be behind someone to strangle them?" Gord looked around. "After the Inspector released the van back to Randy, he showed me where you found Geoff. There's no room behind that seat if it was turned toward the door."

"So, Geoff was strangled, probably from behind," DeAnn said, using her hands to mimic the act of pulling a cord tight. "Then placed in the van seat, and a guitar pick placed in his hand to frame Marius."

Gord snapped his fingers and pointed toward the alley. "What about fingerprints? Would the killer leave prints on the pick?"

"That's a question for the inspector," I said.

Gord raised an eyebrow. "Couldn't you ask your girlfriend?"

"If she's talking to me," I said with a shrug.

"Oh, yeah. I forgot about that Niki girl you told me about." Gord gave me a sympathetic frown. "Have you tried to talk to Courtney?"

"She's kinda busy right now." I couldn't do anything but shrug.

DeAnn filled in what looked like an awkward gap in the conversation. "Did Marius get a good attorney?"

Suki nodded. "We texted a friend of ours who's in the field. He sent a message that someone from his practice was going to Fort Erie tonight to help Marius."

Randy shook his head. "I hope Geoff knows how much he's costing us. Even if he is dead. Attorneys aren't cheap."

DeAnn gave a nod with a reassuring smile. "Well, at least

the attorney will keep him from saying anything incriminating."

"Maybe..." Randy shook his head. "Here in Canada, you have a right to speak with an attorney. But the police can question you without the attorney present. I hope Marius paid attention to the attorney before the interview."

DeAnn paled slightly. "Oh! Ouch! I had no idea laws were so different up here. Does he have an alibi? What happened after the show?"

"Um... What normally happens... drinks with the fans that stay after the last set," Randy shrugged. "We're lucky that Darcy gave us rooms upstairs while we're here. We each got a room of our own, since there isn't much tourist traffic yet."

"Right," Suki added. "Darcy said the guys would have to share a room if we come back for a summer run. Or sleep in the van."

I pinched my lips sideways, trying to piece the events of the night together. "Did anyone see Geoff or Marius go outside after the show?"

Randy blew out a breath. "Geoff has been flighty ever since we hired him. He's got ... um... a key to the van." Randy glanced at the only mundane present, and barely avoided saying *keyed his wand to open the van.*

"Is he a smoker?" I was trying to piece together why the drummer might be outside.

Suki and Randy shared a glance. She added, "No, but he gets messages a lot. No sense in replying where everyone can see you."

"Maybe he went out to make a late night call?" DeAnn suggested. "Courtney should get his phone records and see who he texted and called last night."

Gord and I looked at each other, both understanding what

DeAnn didn't. The messages Suki mentioned were probably magical communications. Fae phones were good, but they left a record. Private messages sent by magic couldn't be traced. And that's the kind of message you didn't want to be noticed sending or receiving.

"So," Suki said, looking at me. "Will you help us? Marius didn't kill Geoff."

"Well... I... uh..."

"We'll get right on it tomorrow!" DeAnn volunteered, including me in that *we*, I was sure.

I sighed and nodded. "I don't know how much help we can be, but I'll see what I can uncover."

A few minutes later, Gord walked with me and DeAnn as we headed home for the night. We dropped DeAnn at her cottage behind Mr. McGristle's house first with a promise to meet for breakfast at Eerie Doughnuts in the morning.

"I'll still be in bed, it's my day off from the shop," Gord reminded me as he walked me to my home. He was two doors down from Mr. McGristle's place, so it wasn't far. I watched him walk to his front door from my front window.

Cleo was curled on my bed and cracked an eye open when I flipped the light in the bathroom on. Ten minutes later, I was in bed with Cleo snuggled in the bend in my knees. Sleep didn't take long.

Nor last long.

A cold paw poked my nose. Several times.

"Wha...ah?" I mumbled and cracked an eye. It was still dark outside. The clock by my bed read three-twelve.

Cleo's paw pressed against my lips.

Quiet. I hear someone outside trying to get in.

12

C rud! That adrenaline spike woke me up fast, as a shiver ran its icy fingers along my spine. We hardly had any late night activity in Eerie Falls. So someone slinking around outside my windows wasn't a good thing. I fought the urge to dive under my bed.

My heartbeat was fast and loud. I swear the wannabe intruder could probably hear it racing. Instead of hiding, I reached for my phone and tapped out a quick message to Courtney.

Cleo says she heard someone outside my windows!

Are you back home yet?

It didn't take long for the response.

No. Still in Fort Erie.

Was going to bunk at the detachment tonight.

You sure you heard someone?

A squeaky scratching sounded from the front rooms. Like someone was rubbing against the glass.

Yes.

I hear it out front.

Someone at the window.

Courtney's reply took a moment. I had no idea what she was doing, so I swung my feet off the bed and into my slippers. T-shirt and exercise shorts were normal sleep attire this time of year. But it was cold outside. What if I had to flee? Should I tiptoe over to the closet and grab my robe.

My phone buzzed with a reply from Court.

I woke Willard up. He'll be there in about five minutes.

My gun safe is keyed to you too.

I left a backup there for just this type of occasion.

Get the 9mm out. The magazine next to it is full.

Slide it in the bottom of the grip.

Pull back the top of the gun and release fast.

That will chamber a round.

Lever by your right thumb - press down to turn the safety off.

I shook my head and tapped another message.

No way am I touching a gun.

Not with my curse.

I'd probably shoot myself or Cleo

Courtney shot back a fast reply.

I'm not there to help. Please get the gun!

I flipped screens and fired off a text to Gord asking for help.

Right! Be there in a flash.

Calling in reinforcements

I wasn't sure who he'd call. Drake Huppe? Mr. McGristle? I tapped my thread with Courtney and typed.

Just texted Gord. He's on his way.

After a couple of beats of my still pounding heart, her reply came through.

Great...

I could hear her sarcasm as I read that. But what could I do? Gramps wasn't close. Willard was on his way. Gord was almost across the street from me. He could be here in a minute.

A book thudded into my lap. Cleo, with her tail upright, must have magicked it from the bookcase in my front room.

Wand out. Make this glyph on the cover to cast the spell.

"What?" I whispered but did as I was told. I'd learned a long time ago to not argue with my grams. She projected an image of a glowing glyph into the air above the book.

"No time to figure it out," I told myself, and shoved magic into my wand. I wasn't sure how much was needed, so I tried to fill myself with energy from the closest ley line. Another scritch from the front room interrupted the pounding of my heart thudding in my ears.

Concentrate! I took a breath and tried to centre my thoughts. Cleo watching me just the way Grams used to whenever she gave me a magic lesson.

Slow down. Take your time with the glyph. The form you draw directs the energy.

Yep. That was Grams in Cleo's tiny body. Exactly what she'd say every magic lesson.

When my now-charged wand touched the book and I drew the symbol she projected, the book flew off my lap. The *Collected Poems of James Whitcomb Riley,* leather-bound special printing, I noted and glanced at the blinds covering the bedroom window. No frost on the pumpkin here. Low temps had been above freezing for more than a week. But it was breezy in my bedroom. Not from an open window, though.

Book after book sailed into the bedroom, and a smaller version of the book golem from our shop formed amid the cyclone of tomes.

Hmmm. I would have thought you'd have more books squirrelled away in here. Oh well. We'll go with this little fellow. Cleo's chuckle accompanied her disapproving observation.

"I have more on my e-reader," I hissed out in a firm whisper. "Not all books are paper now."

"Well, those books won't help right now. This is as big as the golem will get. It will follow and protect you, since you cast the spell." Cleo's voice sounded in my head. *Now let's go see who or what is scraping your window.*

I followed slowly, tiptoeing behind Cleo. She looked back over her shoulder once and waited for me to catch up. Confronting whatever was out there wasn't what I really wanted to do. With the rustle of hardbacks rubbing each other, the stunty book golem, not even as tall as I, shambled behind me. I wasn't sure if it would be much help.

My phone buzzed again. I still carried it in my left hand. Gord this time.

We're right outside.

Don't see anyone.

I wasn't sure who his *we* referred to, but it was nice to not be alone anymore. Another deep breath. Friends had arrived. No longer was I all alone. Well, not counting Cleo, the undead cat, and the shortish book golem. A bit more confident, I flipped on the kitchen light. It spilled into the front room, and I gasped. A large, hairy face peered in at me from the larger window a few feet away from the front door.

Gord's face slid in next to it. Randy the Sasquatch was his backup. Gord pointed towards the door. *Let us in!* He mouthed.

I blew out a breath I didn't know I was holding. Relief flooded through me. I wasn't alone any longer.

I'm right here with you. Cleo's mental voice sounded as if she was repressing a chuckle.

"Stop reading my mind!" I hissed on the way to the door.

I'm not. I'm reading you, Sammi. You wear your emotions very visibly.

With a twist of my hand, the deadbolt rasped back, and I opened the door to Gord holding his wooden handled broom like a martial arts staff. Randy stood next to him, still in the aloha shirt and shorts.

"Came as fast as I could," Randy said, ducking to enter. He still had to duck inside the house. My ceiling was just the normal height. That was about seven feet off the floor, judging by how the Sasquatch had to tilt his head while standing inside.

The sound of pixie wings hummed and darted around the house. After a moment, Willard returned, in small form, flying at eye level.

"Courtney said you heard an attempted entry via a window. Which one?"

Cleo's thought flashed into my mind. *Kitchen.*

I pointed at the appropriate window, and Willard darted off.

"Ummm... What's that?" Gord pointed to the hallway back to the bedroom. He held his broom bristle end forward.

"My little book golem." I shrugged, not sure I wanted to explain about my grams's spirit in the undead cat giving me an emergency magic lesson.

"It's cute," Randy said with a chuckle.

The golem wasn't smart. They never are. It must have interpreted Randy's deep laugh as an aggressive tone and took a step towards him.

"Now, now, little fella." Randy raised his hands, palms out. "I'm a friend. At least I hope I am."

"If you run to my aid in the middle of the night, then you're a friend," I said, flashing him a smile as I waved at the book golem to back up. Then I turned to Gord. "Put your broom down. Whitty isn't a threat if you're nice."

Gord relaxed but tilted his head slightly. "Whitty?"

I chuckled. "Yeah. The book I cast the spell on, the one in the centre of all that is *The Collected Poems of James Whitcomb Riley*. Whitty seems like a good name for it."

"Ohhhh!" Gord drew the syllable out, and it sounded like he had no idea who Riley had been.

Randy chuckled, then launched into the middle of the poem:

They's something kindo' harty-like about the atmusfere
When the heat of summer's over and the coolin' fall is here—
Of course we miss the flowers, and the blossums on the trees,
And the mumble of the hummin'-birds and buzzin' of the bees;
But the air's so appetizin'; and the landscape through the haze
Of a crisp and sunny morning of the airly autumn days
Is a pictur' that no painter has the colorin' to mock—
When the frost is on the punkin and the fodder's in the shock.

"It's one of my favourites," he said when he finished.

"Sounds like a fun poem," Gord said with a roll of his eyes. He pointed at the book golem. "He needs a head. How about a jack o' lantern? Then you could call him Punkin, like the poem."

I shook my head. "Nope. The real Punkin would get grumpy. And he's a pest when he's grumpy."

"Punkin?" Randy lowered himself onto my sofa and stretched his legs out. "What is a punkin? You talk like it's a real person."

I sighed. "A cat. No... a pookah who was turned into a cat by Her Grace."

"You met the fae queen? And her cat?" Randy raised his eyebrows in disbelief.

"Not her cat." I shrugged, but smiled, remembering my time in Wales. "My friend Ebrel has Punkin now. He's her familiar for another century. Ebrel's aunt was miffed when Punkin the pookah um...." How to say it politely. Grams was always grumping when I didn't use polite words with guests. And the tall Sasquatch sprawled on my sofa sure counted as a guest. Coming in at three a.m. to chase off an intruder definitely qualified him as such.

"Punkin ralphed all over the queen's fancy gown," Gord chimed in, laughing. As usual, I stayed polite, and Gord filled in the gross parts. "I so want to meet the fuzzball that honked off her grace."

A rap on the door interrupted. Willard, now in his human-sized form, let himself in and shut the door behind him. He reached into a cargo pocket on the leg of his uniform and pulled out a paper bag with the ghostly logo of Gord's doughnut shop. He plucked out a doughnut hole, then held the bag out to offer some to us. We waved off the gesture.

"Had to get into my emergency stash. That Durand woman ate the box I had in the office earlier." He licked the sugar off his finger.

"You probably should have flown faster and not left her waiting," I said. "You know how those Ottawa government types are."

"I've already texted Courtney. She was burning up my phone with requests for situation reports." He shook his head. "Nothing out there. You've got fresh mulch around the house, and I couldn't find any footprints in it. There are a few scuff marks in the winter glaze of dust and such on all the windows. Maybe a bird trying to get in."

"Or a pixie," Randy added. "Nocturnal birds are hunters. How many owls would try to open a window? Especially if it tried each window?"

Willard nodded. "I didn't want to suspect anyone from our pixie colonies here. They're all good people."

"The same with Zoey," Gord said. "She's the newest pixie in town."

I nodded. "Did she ever get out to meet the Pixie Council?"

Willard shook his head. "Not yet. We on the council will all stop in for lunch at Taps this weekend. She said she'd get someone to cover while she sits for an introductory chat."

"Good," I said. "I've just met her and really like her."

"Well, Darcy is a good judge of character," Willard said with a smile. "Running a bar for a few years gives her insight most people don't realize."

I pointed at the front window. "It probably wasn't a bird. That only leaves pixies."

Willard nodded, but added, "Or one of the even rarer flying fae. Like a bird shifter."

"Those are rare, aren't they?" I pursed my lips to keep from grinning. I knew a bird shifter and looked forward to when she was coming to visit in a few years.

"If it was a pixie trying to break in," Gord said, heading into the kitchen to look at the window. "Can you get any fingerprints off of the window?"

"I can try. In small form, pixie fingers aren't very big. The lines on the prints tend to run together."

Gord rubbed his chin, leaning back against the cabinets. "Sort of like smudges?"

"Exactly. And we've never been able to get a spell to pull the tiny smudges apart enough to read the tiny prints."

"Even if you could do that," Randy added, "wouldn't the pixie need to have been fingerprinted sometime in the past to show up?"

Willard nodded. "Exactly. But a pixie daring enough to break into a house has probably had a few brushes with the Ontario Provincial Police."

My phone buzzed again. A message from Courtney.

You okay?

I hit the reply field.

Yes. Willard, Gord, and Randy are here.

After a second, I typed another line. Time to test the water and see if she was grumpy about that Niki incident.

Miss you!

I smiled when I saw her reply.

Miss you too. Get some sleep.

13

Cleo trotted past me as we neared the doughnut shop. *I suspect we've got another colony of mice moving in. I'll see if I can catch a few before you start clomping around in the bookstore.*

"I do not clomp!" I said, shaking my head. Cleo could use the kitty sized flap into the bookstore's office that I had G'rex install. She and I had keyed it to her undead paw's touch. No other critter could use the kitty door. So no worry about the stray chipmunk or racoon getting in.

I shrugged, watching her for a few seconds, then pulled the door open to Eerie Doughnuts.

DeAnn was already seated. She had a corner table and a paper to-go cup of coffee in front of her. A medium-sized box of ghostly bits, the caramel-flavoured, sugar-coated doughnut holes that the shop specialized in, sat in front of her open. "Sharing!" she said and pointed to the box of holes.

"Sorry I'm late." I flashed her a smile, then headed to the counter. Misty, one of the pixie girls who worked at the shop, filled my travel tumbler for me. With a cup of coffee to make up for my interrupted night's sleep, I turned back towards DeAnn.

The glass door to the shop opened and Courtney strode in. Her eyes flicked around, saw me, and she almost ran the half-dozen steps between us.

Her embrace was tight. I hugged her back, closing my eyes and enjoying the contact. Fortunately, being fae, she didn't need the bullet stopping accoutrements that mundane cops wore. I could feel her warmth through her uniform.

"So glad you're safe," she said quietly into my ear.

"I am too." But I shifted slightly and pulled back. "Hugging you is like hugging Batgirl. Your belt with all those bat-gadgets isn't the most comfortable thing."

"You complaining about hugging me?" Courtney stepped back but took my free hand in hers.

"Not at all." I was grinning silly girl grins but didn't care. Courtney wasn't mad at me, so I was happy. "Come on, I promised DeAnn I'd have breakfast with her."

"Okay, but I can only stay a moment."

She held my hand until we got to the two-seater DeAnn had grabbed.

"So glad you two are happy," the author said with a relieved smile.

Courtney pulled a chair over from the empty table next to DeAnn's. "Why wouldn't we be?"

DeAnn dropped her chin and looked at me.

"What? She's been busy. We haven't talked about Niki's stupid actions yet."

Courtney laughed. "You were worried about that?"

My cheeks warmed, and I nodded, afraid to say anything that might screw this up. Courtney just shook her head.

"I know what Niki is like, and I saw her move her hand to grab yours." Another chuckle from her, and her hand found mine, squeezing it lightly. "And your accidental kick on the table leg was perfect. I'm proud of your quick thinking. She deserved a face full of whatever that was."

"A Cosmo, I believe. And it was an accident. My klutz curse kicked in."

DeAnn bobbed her head in agreement. "It was perfect. And you shouldn't call it a curse since those aren't real. You're just unlucky."

Courtney raised an eyebrow and tilted her head, looking at the author. "Curses are not real, but luck is?"

DeAnn paused for a few seconds. "Oh dear. I see what you mean. Well, perhaps Sammi just has impeccable timing that works in her favour sometimes?"

"We'll go with that," I said.

I tried to stifle a yawn but wasn't successful.

"Late night?" DeAnn asked.

I glanced at Courtney. Her face shifted into her stoic cop look, devoid of emotion.

"Cleo heard someone trying to get into my place last night and woke me up," I said, blowing out a breath. "And my girl-friend with the badge and gun was off in Fort Erie."

"I told you, I left a backup firearm in the gun safe at your house."

"With my klutz cur...." I trailed off, not wanting to rehash the curse vs luck debate. "You know how I am. There is no way I want to hold a gun. I'd shoot the wrong person."

DeAnn nodded support for the idea. "For once, I agree with Sammi. She probably shouldn't ever get a gun."

"Did you ever learn gun safety or how to shoot?" Courtney asked her.

DeAnn nodded. "Of course. The ex loved guns. You know how American men are. We had a membership at the conservation club. I wasn't half bad with a .22 rifle, but I didn't enjoy shooting anything with a larger calibre."

"We've got quite a few gun clubs here in Southern Ontario," Courtney said with a nod toward the outside. "Bert Bowie has applied for the permits to open a skeet range on his land."

DeAnn's brows dropped, and a sideways frown settled on her mouth. "They're far enough out from town? We won't hear all of that banging here, will we?"

Courtney shrugged. "Winter, maybe. Sound carries farther in cold, dry air."

She turned to me and gave a grin. "I loved how you phrased your text last night. That Cleo told you someone was trying to break in. She learn how to speak?"

Court was walking a fine line of inquiry since we had a mundane present. I took her question to be whether Cleo had actually become a familiar animal. A witch's familiar gained human intelligence and a magical ability to speak audibly.

I didn't want to admit Cleo's real nature of housing my grams's spirit and her ability to communicate telepathically. So I shrugged.

"You know how cats are. She's always bopping me on the nose with a paw to wake me up. That's what she did last night."

DeAnn's face blanched. "Oh dear! And that's when you heard someone jiggling your windows or whatever?"

I nodded, thankful that she was filling in with logical suppositions.

"That's one smart cat," Courtney added, then rose.

"Speaking of your windows, I want to run a fingerprint... kit on them."

She'd almost said spell. I chuckled and stood too. "One more hug for the road? You going to be around for lunch?"

"I should be." Her hug ended with a kiss on my cheek. "Gotta get a coffee refill before I go."

DeAnn pushed the box of ghostly bits towards me. I smiled my thanks and plucked one out and waved with that hand at Courtney as she pushed open the door. Her smile disappeared instantly, and she stepped out, holding the door.

Niki Durand pushed past her without even a nod of thanks.

"Do you ever feel the air get sucked out of a room," DeAnn half whispered.

If Niki heard, she didn't say anything.

"Sooooo..." DeAnn leaned in and kept her voice quiet. "Looks like everything is back to normal with you two?"

I shrugged. "I guess. Whoever was jiggling the windows last night probably did me a favour in that regard."

DeAnn closed her eyes and surpassed a shudder. "Not the way I'd want to find out my love life was still on track."

I shrugged and took another doughnut hole out of the box. "Me neither, but I'll take what I can get."

"Ladies! So good to see you this morning." Niki Durand stopped at our table with one of the shop's larger cube shaped boxes of ghostly bits, its top nicely folded and forming a carrying handle. She didn't offer to share her doughnut holes. But I wouldn't have expected it, since we still had a few in DeAnn's smaller box. Instead, she set her to-go cup of coffee on the table next to us, shook about four sugar packets before ripping them open and dumping them in her coffee.

"Still in town?" I asked as she stirred the cup with a wooden stir-stick, not sure how to take her visit.

"Well, another day of auditing the various departments at town hall, then I should be finished." She wore that same political smile again. "And I wanted to apologize for catching you off guard yesterday. I had no idea you'd be so surprised."

"Nothing to worry about." I forced a polite smile on my face, hopefully matching Niki's disingenuous political one. "I hope you were able to dry off okay?"

"Oh yes. Once the bar staff got a towel over." Niki's sarcasm was evident in her tone.

"Well, your timing was perfect," DeAnn added. "No wonder Sammi jerked and kicked the table. You grabbed her hand right as Courtney walked in. Propositioning a girl right as her girlfriend is in earshot."

"Speaking of propositions," Niki's gaze shifted towards DeAnn. "I'd love to hear your input on how this town is performing. Get an outsider's view."

DeAnn raised an eyebrow and paused a moment. "First, you're not my type. Second, I'm afraid that I have words to word today. This book isn't writing itself. I'm not even sure who the killer in the book is."

"Well, at least when that inspector arrived on scene, the investigation moved forward," Niki said, letting her smile shift subtly. "Big city cop does what the little podunk town constable can't. Solve a murder. At least that ... guitarist is in a cell now."

She'd almost let *vampire* slip but had corrected. And her insult to Courtney was anything but veiled. I felt my mood shift to anger.

DeAnn chimed in before I could say anything.

"You know, I think I know what my book is missing. Not

only did I need to add a town gossip, but I also need to add a government flunky. Someone struggling to prove their worth but keeps trying too hard and making enemies wherever she turns."

Niki giggled. "Oh. Sounds like a book I should read." Despite her giggles, her tone was more sarcastic than polite.

"I'll send you an autographed copy. Since you're so interested in the characters." DeAnn's tone matched Niki's.

The special assistant, or whatever she was, spun and headed toward the door. "Good day, ladies."

She pushed right past Drake Huppe, who had just pulled the door open. His shocked look shifted to his lecherous leer as he watched her stalk off.

"She's definitely your type, Drake," I called when he stepped in.

"Female, you mean?" DeAnn asked.

"Bossy and condescending?" I suggested, then shook my head. Drake ignored us and headed towards Misty at the doughnut counter. She glanced our way and rolled her eyes when his gaze settled on the doughnut case behind her.

The door to the shop opened again, and Bob Needles walked in. He waved at me and stood behind Drake, waiting his turn at the counter. Huppe glanced back and flashed Bob a smile. That was enough to get him to stop flirting with Misty and get his order in.

"So..." DeAnn pulled me back with her long syllable. "Did you learn anything about the murder? We've got to figure out who did it."

"Nothing yet. Let me see what the paper says." I opened my phone and logged into my account for the London paper. It was a mundane publication, and probably the safer option with DeAnn across from me. "Oh, this paper doesn't have anything. Rarely do they cover happenings in Eerie Falls."

"Well, the town is fairly small." DeAnn raised her to-go cup for another sip.

"Courtney said they rarely bother to call in and check the police logs. We don't usually have much going on, so they skip us."

"You mean, they only call in when my mother gives them a hot lead?" Bob Needles said and set his tray on the table next to us. "She mentioned they've downsized their staff, and her favourite gossip columnist was made redundant. She's probably miffed at the management and hasn't called them."

DeAnn smiled and took another sip. "How is your mother? I evidently got her miffed at me when I offered to put her in one of my books."

Bob chuckled and flashed a grin. "You definitely need to include her. Every town needs a gossip. And she's secretly thrilled at the prospect. But she won't admit it."

"I've often found that to be the case," DeAnn agreed. "No one wants to admit they desire the attention and notoriety. Even if I change the names. They know it's themselves."

"Well, as her son, you're probably not the target of her gossip and innuendo," I interjected. "At least you get a pleasant visit with her."

"If you call a long list of honey-do chores, including getting her, umm, package from the train, pleasant." He meant her faerock order but couldn't mention it in front of DeAnn.

I took another sip of coffee, trying to hold back a yawn. "How much longer are you staying in town?"

"Just today. I was hoping to catch the band, even without Geoff. But they look to be done for the weekend."

I nodded. "I'd love to catch up more with you, but two late nights in a row is catching up with me."

"I can swing by the bookshop later," Bob suggested. "It's been a while since I added anything new to my bookcase."

"You're supposed to read the books, not just shelve them," I chided him.

"And we're supposed to be solving a murder, remember?" DeAnn suggested.

"You don't think the guitarist is the culprit?" Bob raised an eyebrow and watched DeAnn.

"Of course not. The first suspect the police grab is never the suspect." DeAnn shook her head. "We need Sammi to figure out who the real killer is."

"Well..." Bob trailed off his thought, then leaned forward towards us. He kept his voice low, almost behaving like his mother when she was going to share some juicy gossip. "Take a hard look at Zoey Breeze. She and Geoff had a big row going back in college. Geoff almost got Zoey expelled."

14

That caught me by surprise. "What? Expelled?"

"Yeah. She was, well... Zoey was treasurer of the Drama Club on campus but was going by Joey then. When Zoey got nominated to step up to Vice President of the club, Geoff was dabbling in theatre and took over the finances. About two months later, Geoff went to the president with a bunch of records that didn't match. Accused Zoey of diverting funds and covering it up."

"What happened? Zoey didn't really steal the money, did she?"

"Well, we don't think so." Bob leaned back and took another sip of coffee. "I was on the accounting team that was appointed to dig into the matter. Some records, almost like magic, were missing or suspiciously altered."

That must be Bob's way of letting me know they'd uncovered magical shenanigans about the records.

"And Zoey was suspected?"

"More than just suspected. Geoff outright accused her."

"Oh no. Did she clear her name?"

"Barely. But yes." Bob blew out a breath. "It took me a while to crack the spell of deception on those records. There were shenanigans, but neither Geoff nor Zoey could be proven to have altered the records. Both were requested to provide their own personal financial information. Zoey immediately complied. We had to threaten to turn the matter over to the provincial police to get Geoff to cooperate. But the audits of both were clean. Nothing out of the ordinary that we could trace back to being embezzled funds from the Drama Club."

DeAnn shook her head and blew out a breath of disbelief.

"Oh. I can see why Zoey might carry a grudge against him. And he thought he could have the audacity to get handsy with her at the pub here in town."

"That's definitely Geoff's style. He'll chase everyone in a skirt, even if he honked them off or accused them of embezzlement a decade before."

"Yeah, but is either a reason for Zoey to want to kill Geoff?" DeAnn shook her head. "I mean, Geoff didn't actually get her expelled, did he?"

"Not expelled, no." Bob shook his head. "But the drama of the embezzled funds took her out of the running to play Hamlet. That's all she was talking about. I've never seen anyone so mad. She actually punched Geoff and knocked him off his feet. That was after college officials told Zoey that she wasn't being considered for any roles until the money matters were cleared."

"Zoey punched someone?" I was shocked. "She so doesn't seem like the personality that would resort to violence."

"Well, this was pre-transition, remember? There might have been some testosterone fuelling that punch." Bob shrugged. "Geoff was spitting mad. Had a black eye for over two weeks. That almost got Zoey expelled, but it happened off campus. Evidently Geoff was making a big deal about how he got Zoey banned from the production right before the fist and eye connection occurred."

I leaned back in my chair, thinking. "Was anyone arrested for the altercation? I hate to consider Zoey, but I want to make sure the wrong person isn't in jail for killing that drummer."

Bob thought for a moment, then nodded. "I think Geoff pressed charges against Zoey. But if you look it up, remember she changed her name after that occurred."

DeAnn had her lips scrunched sideways and tapped a finger on the table. "But is that enough motive to kill the cad now? I mean, that was several years ago, right?"

"About a decade, maybe twelve years?" I said and looked at Bob for the exact date.

"Eleven, if my memory serves."

"You're an accountant," I chuckled. "Numbers and dates have always been your thing."

He shrugged but smiled. "Well, that's about all I'm good at right now. The bank account is comfortable, and I can stay in Toronto, away from Mother and her gossip club."

DeAnn drummed her fingers on the table, staring off past me, then took the last doughnut hole out of the box. After biting it in half, she used it to point toward Eerie Taps. "But why would Zoey need to kill Geoff now? Ten-year-old revenge for not getting the lead in Hamlet."

"That role has been one of her dreams," I said, remembering our walk back from picking up the faerock orders. "I don't get the read on her that she'd kill a decade or so after it."

"Yeah. Giving someone a black eye is probably the worst that would be justified in that case."

Bob tilted his cup back, draining the last of his coffee. "She and Geoff ran into each other often in Toronto, according to what she told me over at Darcy's bar. Why wait until she gets to a small place like this to do him in?"

"Good point," I added. Despite my inclinations against Marius as the perp, he was the logical choice.

DeAnn stared at me for a few seconds. "You're thinking Marius really did it?"

"Well, who are the suspects?" I turned my hands palm up and shrugged. "Marius attacked him in Taps, when Geoff groped Suki."

"But there is also Suki and Randy. He's a big guy and protective of Suki."

Bob shook his head, rising. "I'll leave mystery solving to you two. If numbers aren't attached, I'm out of my element."

"Bye, Bob. I'll be at the bookstore, except for a late lunch," I said.

"I'll stop in after I see what else Mother has lined up for me."

Once Bob had left, DeAnn leaned forward. "Well?"

"Well, what?"

She tilted her head toward the table next to us, where Bob had sat. "What about him? Giving us distractions, so we don't focus on him. Was he doing any loansharking at college or after? Geoff could have been in the hole, and Bob's your uncle!"

I tilted my head, puzzled. "The Needles family, and the Cupertinos are not related that I know of."

DeAnn laughed. "No, the old saying. Bob's your uncle, means something is obvious."

"Ohhhhh! Sorry."

"Think about it," DeAnn said. "Bob follows the band down here to his former hometown. Geoff ends up dead the next morning."

"Well, there's Niki Durand too. She shows up at the same time as both of them. Even earlier, in fact. She was with Lorne before the band arrived."

"So, we've got three band members with motives," DeAnn said and raised three fingers. Then raised the fourth and her thumb. "Five, when we add Bob and Niki."

"Well, if you're looking at suspect pool only from those who attended college with Geoff, add in Courtney. But she wouldn't kill him."

"Are you sure? Did she say anything to make you think she might harbour a grudge against him?"

"What? No!"

DeAnn flashed a smile of apology. "Sorry. Just making sure."

"Look, it's Courtney's job to find the murderer, not ours," I almost growled, then suppressed another yawn. "Wow, these late nights are catching up with me."

"And to think you had a prowler almost break into your place last night." DeAnn shivered, wrapping her arms across her chest. "If I had a car, I'd be locking it. And I'll probably butt a chair in front of my door tonight."

"Yeah. Eerie Falls usually only gets a wild teenager prank or two. Never a break in. Most people don't even lock their cars." Another yawn pushed its way through my coffee and sugar buzz.

"You better take a nap soon," DeAnn suggested, "or you won't be awake for lunch with the girlfriend."

"I've got to work the bookstore." I yawned again.

"Call your grandfather and get him to come in early." She stared at me, daring me to disagree.

I blew out a long breath and nodded, pulling out my phone to text Betty. "What are you doing today?"

"Well, I've got to get my morning words in. That book isn't writing itself." She swirled her cup, then tilted it back. "After I get my five-thousand words for the day, I'll head over to the yarn store. See if I catch any good gossip."

"You sure it's safe for you and Mrs. Needles to be around each other?"

"On a Saturday it is. She's leading the knitting clinic, and her counter girl stays out front helping people. Maggie is just as big of a gossip as Lenora is but nicer."

I shook my head and chuckled. "You're as bad as Lenora, always looking for gossip."

"Not gossip, silly." She laughed. "Story ideas."

We parted ways after each getting a coffee refill. I got a box of ghostly bits, just to get a sugar buzz going. I even gave my coffee an extra squirt from the honey bear. Not pixie levels, but I'd need the caffeine and sugar to make it long enough for Gramps to get in and take over the shop. My phone buzzed with a message from Betty. She said to give them two hours.

That was understandable. Gramps was not an early riser and was grumpy when he did get up.

At the shop, I ran through my normal routine and got everything opened. It was only when I perched on the stool behind the front counter and opened the overnight orders that another yawn hit. I reached for the doughnut holes right as the bell on the front door jingled.

Bubbles, the werebear owner of Bear's Cabins, and another man entered.

"Sammi Cupertino, this is Chief. He's going to help me out at the cabins, so I can get some time on my bike this summer." Bubbles waved a meaty hand to the other fellow. I recognized him as the man Bubbles had been sitting with at the bar. He still wore his ball cap with the navy logo and the outline of a ship filled in with grey thread.

"Chief?" I held out my hand. The fellow took it, and the tingle of fae magic lit up the touch. I returned the magical signature. Each indicating fae, but nothing special, like troll, pixie, or any of the other magical races.

"Chief Petty Officer, first class," the man said. "Real name is Cobie Marcus."

"Isn't it unusual for a fae to serve in the Royal Canadian Navy?"

Bubbles chuckled and dropped into one of the easy chairs. "He's been hearing that a lot."

Chief parked on the stool across the counter from me, his back straight. One hand touched his hat. "Served on the HMCS Bacon Ridge. We were a fae-only ship in World War II, on anti-magic patrol in the North Atlantic. Darn Nazis were always using magic to track the convoy heading to Britain."

"Chief was cox'n on the ship," Bubbles called.

"Cox'n? I'm not up on naval terms."

Chief gave me a smile. "Technically a coxswain is the top enlisted man or woman on the vessel. We are in charge of keeping the boat ready to go. When the captain gets orders to sail, he notifies the coxswain, and we roust the crew. That way, the old man doesn't have to hear the grumbles and the cursing."

"Sailors really curse a lot?"

Bubbles let out a loud rumble of a laugh. "My bike club

hangs around Chief just to learn new cadences of swearing. Nobody curses as well as a Chief Petty Officer."

Another yawn leaked through my defences, and I plucked a doughnut hole out of the box. Then I pushed it toward Chief. "Finish those for me, please. I've had too many."

"That's the other thing sailors do well," Chief said with a grin and pulled one of the doughnut holes out of the box. "We know how to eat."

"Other than working for Bubbles, what brought you to Eerie Fall, Chief Marcus?"

"Just Chief, please Ma'am."

"Then I'm just Sammi."

"Deal, Sammi." He flashed me a smile and took another doughnut hole, holding up with a questioning look. "You sure? I told you sailors know how to eat."

"Please." I gave him a nod, then stifled a yawn.

"You up late again, Sammi? The band didn't play that long last night." My werebear friend grinned and pulled one of the books off the chair. "Not with the guitarist getting arrested for killing the drummer. The one before Gord, I mean."

"About time someone clocked that little twerp," Chief growled. "Whoever did Geoff Gage in, did the world a favour."

𝕾 15 𝕾

My desire for sleep fled, and I raised an eyebrow.

"Sounds like there's no love lost between you and the deceased drummer?"

Chief let out a sound that was closer to a snort than a grunt. "After his daddy did everything he could to destroy my career..." He shook his head and stared off through the front window for a moment.

Bubbles looked up from the book he held. "Was that the fellow that got you assigned to Newfoundland?"

"To the most boring desk job imaginable." Chief glanced over at me. "After the Bacon was retired–"

"You don't retire bacon," Bubbles said with a chuckle. "You eat bacon."

"Ignore Chuckles the bear, Ma'am," Chief said with a roll of his eyes. "When the HMCS Bacon Ridge was mothballed after the war, I moved to a liaison position between the Fae Court and the Royal Canadian Navy. My job included watching for new recruits on the mundane side that might have fae lineage. We had magic sensors installed in the various training centres."

Bubbles snorted a laughed. "And you caught that drummer fellow trying to sneak through as a mundane. I remember now. Honked off his daddy to no end."

"His father is a Canadian Senator, unfortunately. And fae. And heir to the family that invented some of the spells used in the Infernal brand cauldrons." Chief shook his head. Every fae knew that the Infernal brand of magical containment cauldrons were the best at containing the little demons we used. "None of that should have mattered. The treaty between the crowns, Fae and Canadian, say that all fae candidates to the armed forces of Canada must be approved by the Fae Ministry prior to acceptance into the Royal Military College or their enlistment in the tri-forces. Geoff was trying to sneak into the RNC as a mundane after being denied by the Fae Ministry."

"He thought his daddy's name would take him places," Bubbles said, stretching his legs out and clasping his hands behind his head in a lounging position. His frame was already large, and I was glad that Grams had long ago added oversized chairs to the seating area.

"Well, Senator Gage had a right fit that his son had to stand in front of an admiral for about half a day, in his cadet uniform, answering questions. Finally, the admiral told him to remove the uniform and get his, um, rear end off the campus and out of the service." Chief blew out a breath. "The admiral told me we'd both catch political heck over it. He had his next star delayed. I got posted to a dead end post. But I'd do it all over again. Don't besmirch my navy with shenanigans just because you think your daddy is important."

"Well, now you know what will happen," Bubbles chided

his friend. "If you want to go sit in Northern Newfoundland and watch paint dry on the walls, the fastest way is to honk off a senator."

"Wait a minute?" I didn't normally pay attention to mundane politics, but I knew we had a few fae MPs and Senators in the Canadian Parliament. "Senator Gage is related to the people behind the Infernal brand of cauldrons in all of our fae vehicles?"

Chief nodded. "And just about every other use for an Infernal cauldron. The last time a company tried to develop a similar product, they couldn't even house a grade three infernal. The demonic doggy inside broke loose and ate the CEO, then chased the staff around the warehouse a dozen times. Fortunately, the King's Company was in the area and raced in."

Bubbles laughed. "Oh, I bet that was fun. Well, except for the guy who got eaten by the infernal."

"Oh, there was buckshot damage to the entire facility." Chief chuckled. "I got to work with Lieutenant Colonel Reece on a mission once. He and his elephant musket can take on a grade five or six infernal if need be."

His story made me perk up. "I got to meet the Lieutenant Colonel. My friend Ebrel knows him."

"Ebrel Dymestl?" Chief peered at me through narrowed eyes as I nodded. "You are friends with a niece of Her Grace?"

I nodded. "Ebrel and I solved the mystery of the Marocchino Sparrow. Rhodri was charming but a bit scatterbrained, as I recall."

"That would be him," Chief said and grinned. "His magical pockets are full of knick-knacks and snacks. I'm surprised he didn't pull out an entire marching band on mission."

"Oh dear, I suppose he could." I chuckled, but that turned

into a yawn. My brain was sluggish but still awake enough to realize I should be suspicious. "You, um... didn't talk to the Inspector about Geoff's murder, did you?"

"Why should I?" Chief narrowed his eyes again, watching me. "I didn't kill him."

"Sammi is dating our town's constable," Bubbles explained. "And she solved the last murder we had in town. She's sharp, when she's not tired."

"Well, I was up at three this morning because someone tried to break into my house!"

Bubbles cocked his head, a look of concern washing over his face. "Why would they do that? Someone trying to steal one of your books again?"

"I have no idea," I said and yawned again. "I wish Gramps would hurry up. I need a nap before Courtney stops by."

"Hmmm..." Bubbles stroked his chin. "Chief and I will drive by your place tonight and tomorrow on our way home. Just to look for anyone suspicious."

"Thanks," I said but didn't feel comforted, not knowing if I could trust Chief or not. Bubbles I trusted. I hoped his trust in the new guy was warranted.

"We should be going," Bubbles said, rising. "I want to introduce Chief to all the merchants in town."

"That's probably a good move, as small as Eerie Falls is," I said, then chuckled. "Did you warn him about Mrs. Needles?"

"That he did," Chief said and flashed a broad smile. "I'll win her over with my sailor's charm."

"You mean your sailor's cursing." Bubbles laughed and stepped towards the door.

I shook my head. Chief did have a pleasant smile, and I liked him after just a few minutes. But, with Mrs. Needles, I wasn't sure. "You'd better learn how to gossip and to knit if you want on her good side."

"No time for knitting, unfortunately," Chief said with a chuckle. "Bubbles has been slow on his repairs to those cabins. I've already got a list that will keep us busy throughout the summer. And Chief Petty Officers don't gossip if they want to retain their rank."

"Well, good luck with Mrs. Nee—" another yawn took over.

Bubbles paused at the door, hand on the knob. "You said you're going to lunch with Courtney?"

"I hope. Depends on if she gets a call."

"If you're going to Darcy's pub, we'll try to time it so Chief can meet Constable Courtney then. Lorne should be back on Monday, so we'll come back in then."

"Two cops in this town?" Chief grinned. "You didn't tell me the town was big enough for two cops."

"We just got a real stoplight in town. We might get another one in the next decade."

Bubbles and Chief had no sooner left than the bell on the door jingled yet again. I tried my best to keep my smile straight when Lenora Needles walked in.

"Ah. Sammi. Just who I was looking for."

"Did you expect Gord to be running my shop? Or Darcy?" I wasn't normally that snarky with the town gossip, but another yawn leaked through. Being tired must make me cranky. Or at least snarky.

Mrs. Needles set her oversized bag on our counter, the red yarn and blue knitting needles still protruding from the un-closed top. I wasn't sure if she'd ever pulled the zipper closed on that bag. It was always stuffed with knitting projects. She dusted the side of the bag with her hand several times.

"Apologies. I didn't mean to get sugar on your counter. But that woman from Ottawa was in. Must have come straight from the doughnut shop. Still had that ghastly caramel-sugar on her fingers. I didn't realize it and asked her to pass me my bag since I was on the way to see you."

"We haven't gotten any new needlecraft books in trade," I said with a nod at the back room. "You know I'll email you when we do."

"Of course. And it's so good of you to let me purchase them at your cost."

Letting the knitting shop have all the used stock on needle crafts like knitting and crochet was my way of keeping the town gossip from stopping in every morning to snoop around. Once I'd taken over running the store when Grams got sick, that was one of the first executive decisions I made. It saved the little bit of sanity Gramps and I had left while dealing with the doctors and hospital visits for Grams.

That was a decision I should have made, Cleo's thought drifted into my mind. *But it was too fun to snipe at her every time she came in. At least until I became ill. Then even that joy was too much trouble to continue.*

I glanced over at Cleo, crouched low, staring at a corner of where a bookcase met the wall. Cleo's tail twitch told me she sensed a rodent interloper in the shop. I resisted the urge to sigh as I turned back to Mrs. Needles.

"You said you wanted to see me?" Why was she here?

Mrs. Needles looked around, probably hoping there was a bigger audience to share whatever her juicy news was.

"Well, you know my Robert is in town. I do so wish I could get him to settle down here in Eerie Falls." She straightened slightly and smiled. "This town needs a great accountant. You probably get so flustered keeping track of your taxes."

"I get by okay," I said. Which was true. The software tracking our sales and inventory was not complicated. But I dare not let Gramps do anything other than enter sales. He was too absentminded to keep up with adding inventory to the system.

"Well, think of how much easier with Robert around to keep the financial side running smoothly."

"You know Robert and I are not likely to date, right?"

Mrs. Needles waved a hand dismissively. "Oh, pish, dear. Of course I know that. But I've been keeping my eye out for single young ladies that might like an attractive accountant in their dating lives."

I sucked in a deep breath, afraid of where this conversation might be leading.

The town gossip didn't wait for me to ask another question. "That Durand woman came around this morning asking about Robert. He was already out running errands for me. She said they knew each other from their time in university."

"There you go," I said adding what I hoped was a comforting smile. "Niki Durand might be Bob's type of woman. Did she seem interested?"

Not that I'd wish Niki Durand onto any of my friends. But discussions with Mrs. Needles seldom went anywhere useful. I was hoping a real customer might enter and give me an excuse to beg off the conversation with her.

"That woman is pursuing a career in Ottawa. She'll likely run for office herself, and she's from the Hamilton area. That's not Eerie Falls, now is it? Robert wouldn't be here with me if I got those two connected."

With my sleep-deprived brain, I wasn't making sense of where she was going. "I don't see what I can do to help you?"

"Well, to cut to the chase, dear. You know that new girl at that vampire's bar?"

"You mean Zoey, who just started working at Eerie Taps?" Now wasn't the time to educate Mrs. Needles about her implied pejoratives about Darcy's nature. I'd probably take a tone with her that I shouldn't.

"Of course, that young woman. Robert said he knew her from their time at university. But... I've heard..." She leaned in and dropped to a whisper. "That she is a... Lesbian."

16

I blinked several times, debating if I should make a scene and boot the gossip from my store. Since no one else was around to hear what she said, nor the insulting tone in which she said it, I decided to ride the conversation out.

I leaned forward and held a hand to my mouth as though I were about to whisper a secret.

"So am I, Lenora. Courtney and I both are."

"Well, um.... Of course you are, dear." Mrs. Needles' cheeks flared scarlet. "I didn't mean anything by my words."

"Ummmm hmmm..." Again, my voice came through much snarkier than it normally would have been if I weren't so tired.

"Well... I mean, I only stopped here to get your read on the new girl." Mrs. Needles pulled her bag off the counter, holding it with both hands in front of her like she wanted a barrier between her blundering about and my corrections. "I was hoping to hear from you as to whether what I'd heard about this Zoey woman was correct."

"Zoey and Darcy are dating," I replied, sure I wasn't spilling any secrets since they'd been open with their affection. "I really wouldn't suggest you try to set Robert up with anyone. He's capable of finding his own dates."

A soft thud sounded from near the bookcases. Cleo on the pounce.

Mrs. Needles set her bag on the floor and took a half step to the counter, her hands out, palms up. "Oh, I hope you weren't thinking I was trying to set you up with Robert. Your grandmother let me know in very certain terms that you were not his type at all."

I took a deep breath and let it out slowly, counting to ten. If she was this bumbling about dealing with my love life and who I was attracted to, I didn't want her to learn about Zoey for a long while.

She did pay attention to me on occasion. Of course, when I had to set the entire inventory of her store to attack her until she agreed to stop trying to change you just to date her son.

That made me roll my lips in to keep from chuckling. I could only imagine Grams, glowing with magic, making skeins of yarn fly out of their baskets to pelt Mrs. Needles. Grams was always very protective of me.

"Look, Lenora," I said, keeping my tone soft. "Let Bob handle his own love life. Trying to steer someone else into loving who you want them to never works out. Both people are always miserable."

"Well, that wasn't really what I was trying to do—"

"Yes, you WERE!" I let anger show in my voice. Maybe if I weren't so danged tired right now, I might have been more diplomatic. "Let Bob be himself. Did you ever consider that he wants to be in Toronto? Close enough to visit but not be under your thumb all the time."

I almost slapped a hand to my mouth after that came out.

"Well, I never!" Lenora Needles's cheeks flared red, and her brow dropped as she stared at me.

Good line, Sammi. Give the old witch a dose of strong medicine! Cleo had walked back to the front counter, probably to drop her mouse kill into the bin next to me. But I didn't want to look down and give Mrs. Needles a break. I kept my gaze levelled right at her until she blinked and looked off towards the front door. Good. She was considering her escape route.

"Why don't you try listening to your son?" I suggested with my voice firm. "See what he wants and help him get that."

"I'm sorry I even stopped in." She grabbed her bag off the floor and thrust her arm through the two handles. "I've got a knitting class to teach. Good day, Samantha!"

I watched the door swing shut behind her.

"What did I do that for?" I leaned forward, elbows on the counter, head in my hands. "Making an enemy of her is NOT what I need right now."

I hope she enjoys the present I dropped into her bag.

My eyes narrowed, and I leaned over to look at Cleo.

"You didn't!"

That old witch deserves it. Poor Robert.

I glanced at the wastebasket under the counter. No little furry mouse carcass was present.

"You really did..." I tipped my head back and chuckled until another yawn took over.

Gramps showed up about five minutes later. Rather than stagger home, I asked him to get whatever he needed out of the upstairs office.

"Go ahead, Sammi." He waved me on. "Betty said you had a prowler around your place last evening. Tell me about it after you get some sleep. You know where the afghan and pillow are."

Gramps often used the sofa in his office for napping. Enough so that I rotated pillows and some of the afghans Grams had crocheted between my house and his office on a bi-weekly basis.

"Thanks. Only wake me if Courtney shows up or the building catches fire."

You and I recharged the extinguisher spells with the last batch of faerock, dear. Cleo followed me up the stairs. *Your grandfather left too many spells to dwindle to mere nothing. We were fortunate that this kitty had terrible timing with Drake Huppe's truck. Your grandfather could have had flood, fire, famine, and a plague of locusts all descend on the shop and never look up from his research.*

I didn't reply. Instead, I moved a stack of Gramps's latest research tomes off the sofa, spun the handle on the blinds to darken the room, and pulled the pillow and afghan out. A moment later, I was on my side, glasses and phone set on the small table in front of the sofa, and an afghan draped over me. This one was forest green with lighter green and tan accents. No ripple afghans, with their triangular waves, ever emerged from Grams's hooks. That was the only crochet class Lenora Needles taught at her shop. Grams made a point to always crochet better than Mrs. Needles, who preferred to knit.

Of course, dear. I wasn't about to let that snooty snoop be the best witch with a crochet hook. Cleo snuggled into the crook behind my knees.

"Are you reading my mind?" I mumbled. Slumber was only a moment away.

Not at all, dear. Go to sleep.

The little wooden table next to the sofa erupted in a wave

of vibrations. I sat up, blinking. Earthquake? We didn't get those very often.

The table gave a low hum and another wave of vibrations hit. I grabbed my phone, which was dancing across the wood vibrating with a text alert, and squinted, trying to read the text.

It was from Courtney, so I grabbed my glasses.

Wanna meet for lunch soon?

A glance at the time. Gads! It was two hours after I had laid down. Cleo stretched on the couch, pushing both front paws to touch my leg.

Sure, I texted back.

Just woke from a nap.

Give me 15?

Courtney's reply didn't take long. *Meet you at the bookstore.*

I hit the restroom on the way to the front. It wasn't large and rarely used by clients. But I kept a few makeup spell crystals hidden behind the mirror. I even kept a toothbrush back there.

A few moments later, my mouth minty fresh with most of the sleep deprived aura gone from my face, I headed to the front of the bookshop.

Courtney was already there, seated across from Gramps, a cup of coffee with a lid by her elbow. She stood when I walked in and held her hands out. A quick kiss, but no hug since she was still in uniform wearing her bat-belt full of bat-gadgets or whatever the OPP gave her. And with Gramps right there, a kiss was about all the public displays of affection I was comfortable with. After a glance up at me, he turned back to the book on his lap. He'd gotten the research bug again, and even Betty was rolling her eyes about him reading at every chance.

Courtney and I, still holding hands, headed for the door.

"Back in an hour-ish, Gramps," I called. "Take care of Cleo for me."

"Cleo? Oh, your cat. Is she here?"

"Upstairs on the sofa."

"Excellent. Did you know that in 1138 BCE, Diophacles the Elder began a..."

I let the door shut behind us. Courtney led me to the corner to cross, even though we were right across from the pub, and there was rarely traffic on the street. Still, if your girlfriend is the town constable, best not to jaywalk with her.

Inside the bar, several tables and a few stools were occupied with patrons. We waved at Zoey, working the bar, and grabbed a booth.

"Did you find any fingerprints on my windows?" I asked once Zoey had taken our orders.

Court pursed her lips, then reached into a pocket. Out came a small plastic bag, with *Evidence* stamped on it.

"No, but I found this under one of the windows."

Inside was something I didn't recognize at first.

"Is that ... part of a pixie wing?"

The bit of gossamer was flat and curved and sparkled with hints of blue and red.

Courtney nodded and slid the bag back into her uniform pocket. "I showed it to Willard. He said the only time he's seen wing damage like that is when pixies fight. Often with a bird in mid-flight."

"What about when they moult and grow new wings?"

"That's a full wing, according to Willard. Pixies get a week or so walking everywhere while the new wings grow in."

Zoey darted back in pixie form. I caught a glimpse of her wings before she popped tall. Green and purple were the predominant colours in her wings. So it was unlikely to have been her banging around my windows last night.

"If you're wondering about moulting, it sucks," Zoey said, and set our drink order on the table. "Fortunately, we can tell when our wings get brittle right up at the shoulders. I start walking and stay in my tall form when that happens. A day later, no wings." She laughed and shrugged. "Nothing makes a pixie grumpier than losing their wings." Zoey popped pixie and flew off to wait on another table.

"So, you heard someone trying to get in?" Courtney asked.

"Cleo did," I said.

"That's the second time you mentioned Cleo telling you something." She stared at me.

"She's a peculiar cat," I said and shrugged. "We're learning how to read each other. Nothing like being awakened at three a.m. by a nervous cat bopping my nose with her paws."

"Yeah... she's a peculiar cat all right."

"So," I said, hoping to change the direction of the conversation away from Cleo's nature. "What do you think was going on last night with my windows? Was it more than a bird?"

Courtney patted the pocket where she'd stowed the evidence bag. "Definitely more than a bird. Willard didn't notice it last night, but there are small spell scorch marks around your windows. Someone was trying to force a magical entry past your warding spells."

"Small scorch marks? And you found part of a gossamer wing?"

"Caught in a bit of the wood trim around the window. The window over your kitchen sink needs some attention, fortunately." Courtney flashed a smile.

"I asked G'Rex to come out and do some touchup sanding

and painting, but he said wait until summer when he's got a grand-gnome or two helping him."

"Well, we're fortunate that he waited."

Zoey showed up again and popped tall to set our sandwiches in front of us.

Courtney's phone chimed with a tone I knew it was the official alert. She grabbed it and scrolled, reading whatever the alert was.

"Can I get that boxed up?" she asked Zoey. "Gotta run."

"Sure. No problem!" The pixie grabbed her plate, popped tiny, and darted back to the kitchen.

"Not another murder, is it?" I asked, disappointment showing on my face, which I couldn't help. This was my first chance to be alone with Court for almost a day.

"Well, the Inspector's message said it already hit the Fort Erie Times, so I can share." She flipped the screen around and showed me the headline from the news site:

Faerock Train Robbed

Three bags of the mineral missing, believed to have been stolen!

17

"Hey Sammi!"

Gord walked into the bookshop about an hour after I'd returned alone from my lunch.

"Hey Gord. You look happy. They release Marius so you can play tonight?"

He shook his head but kept smiling. "Not yet. Randy and Suki said Marius has a great attorney, and he might be out tomorrow. They're pushing for an emergency hearing to show the judge that the evidence is circumstantial at best."

"You're happy about him staying in jail for another day?" I was kind of caught up on sleep, but that still didn't make sense as to why my friend was happy.

"No. I got Randy and Suki to agree to doing some jazz tunes tonight. Guitar is not needed as critically as it is for rock and roll."

"Ahhhhh...." That made sense. "What time are you guys starting?"

"Six. Darcy said we could give it a try. But if her Saturday

141

night patrons grump, we'll have to wing it on playing rock without a guitar player."

"Can you do that? I mean, most rock has strong guitar presence."

"Yeah..." Gord trailed off and shrugged. "Randy has been working on lead guitar parts and playing the bass part with his pedals. But, well..."

"He has big feet and small pedals?"

Gord nodded slowly. "He wasn't set up for that. He said it's a challenge and doesn't know how drummers do two kick drums and keep our hands moving all the time."

"I can't carry a tune in a bucket, let alone do what any of you do." I shook my head, trying to imagine how bad I'd be in a band.

"That's why you do all the book reading and thinking," Gord said with a huge grin. "I can always count on Sammi to deliver the thoughts and knowledge."

"Well, my thoughts are to let DeAnn know you're going to be jazzing it tonight. I might as well get a partner for dinner, so you've got a few friendly faces listening to your jazz tonight."

"You don't get a Courtney date?"

I shook my head and blew out a breath that was mostly a sigh. "She got a notice about the train robbery and had to run. She texted to say it was going to be another long night."

"Train robbery? When and where?"

"You didn't check the news alerts? *Fort Erie Times* sent out an alert about it."

He shook his head. "We've been jamming, trying to get into a jazz groove. Which we fell into real well." Gord's face lit up as he talked about the music. "If it weren't for helping with Mom's shop, I'd love to tour like they do."

My heart sank, even as I tapped on the laptop at the front counter. "Did Suki or Randy ask you to go with them?" I'd be happy for him, but Gord and I had been best friends for a few decades now. I didn't want him to be gone all the time.

"No, not yet," Gord said, glancing over at Taps. I could hear the wistful tone in his response.

"Here," I tapped the counter to get his attention. "The Fort Erie Times says that the faerock gnomes on the train ran a standard inventory count when they arrived in Fort Erie today. Three of their standard sized bags of faerock were missing. Their last inventory was in Windsor."

"Makes sense. Inventory when they cross the border. Or under it, if I remember right."

I scanned the story on the Times' website. "Yep. They crossed via the Canadian Pacific's Detroit tunnel under the river. Part of the border report was an inventory check and audit."

"Hmmm... How big is a standard sized bag of faerock?"

I shrugged and kept reading. "According to this, a single bag can fuel twenty grade-three sized Infernal engines for almost five years under normal driving conditions."

"Wow!" Gord closed his eyes and shivered, crossing his arms over his chest. "Who, other than a gnome, would want to carry that much faerock around?"

"Not anyone I know, that's for sure." I, too, had to repress a shiver as I glanced back at the office. I'd put the bag of faerock for the shop back there until I had the chance to go recharge all the major spells.

Gord shook his head to clear it and must have noticed my glance back toward the safe where I'd stored our small bag of faerock. "Yeah, if it weren't for needing to feed the ovens and fryers at Mom's shop, I'd just get the expensive recharge crystals and let other witches worry about playing with faerock. Did you ever get Whitty's big brother recharged?"

"Not yet. Cleo and—" I cut myself off, trying to figure out how to recover from almost admitting that Cleo was more than just a normal vampire cat.

"Yeah. Let her finish ridding the shop of mice first," Gord filled in his interpretation of my screw-up.

We'll get to that this next week, dear. And we'll make the golem spell I had you cast at your house into a more stable and permanent enchantment. And with Courtney almost living with you, we should devote a bit of that faerock to enlarging your closet spells. You could use more room the way she's bringing clothing in each time she spends the night.

I glanced over at Cleo, lounging on the back of the chair opposite Gord. She was fastidiously licking a paw and wiping her face.

"Where were you guys practising today? I mean, I was at the bar and didn't see anyone on the stage."

"In the back of the van," Gord said with a grin. "Suki has been working on enlarging the inside-out spell on it. She said Geoff gave it a tweak on the trip down to Eerie Falls. She watched him and got pointers about the spell. He'd wanted to set up his kit inside for jam sessions when they were between gigs."

I tilted my head in question at his statement. "But the drums are still on stage."

"Randy and I moved mine over and into the van when I pressed them to do a jazz night." His face lit up. "I mean, I love gigging with them, and the jazz idea was a good way to make it keep happening. Suki just used her back up keyboard, and Randy had a second bass he brought out."

"You really are considering leaving Eerie Falls!" I shook my head, torn between being happy that Gord was considering following a dream and that my bestie was thinking of leaving town.

Gord just shrugged. "It would be great if they asked me, but I don't know if I can leave Mom and her shop. Although..."

"What?" I dreaded whatever he was thinking. Losing Gord to a life on the road wasn't what I'd thought today would bring. He was a part of my morning routine, and afternoon, and a lot of my evenings.

"Well... I mean... Randy and Suki haven't even asked me."

"Yet," I interjected. "Yeah. That might happen. You were jamming real well with them last night."

Gord shrugged. "Well, if it does, and I go on the road with them, then I won't have to listen to Mom trying to set me up with every eligible girl that comes through town."

"No..." I thought for a second and chuckled. "She'll be calling you every afternoon to ask how many girls you met and when you're bringing one by the doughnut shop to meet her. She wants grandkids. And you're her only hope."

"Ugh! She will do that, won't she?" Gord shivered. "When will she learn I'm just not interested in that?"

I shrugged, unable to answer.

Gord let out a large sigh. "Let's talk about something fun! Who do you think stole the faerock from the train?"

"A train robbery is fun?"

He chuckled and shrugged. "More fun than me dating some girl so Mom can get grand babies."

"I see your point. But..." I shrugged and stared off for a moment. "It would take a lot of planning and work to get past the gnomes and all their security precautions and steal three large bags of faerock. Even with the shielding spells the gnomes have in place, that's a lot of magical power in three bags. You won't be having any grandkids if you're exposed to that for long."

"Ugh, yeah. I mean, they mine most of the rock out of Southern California. The town close to the faerock mine always has birth defects popping up. I read that they've got an insane asylum there for mundanes and fae who get too big of an exposure."

That triggered a memory for me. "Nia, the pixie who works at Mystic Brews in Wales, says she has a cousin in Southern California with a gimpy wing because of faerock exposure."

Gord shivered again. "Faerock is nasty stuff. Who would have the resources to pull off a heist despite the risks?"

I leaned forward, thumb under my chin, tapping a finger on my lips. "That really sounds like organized crime."

"Well, you said that wereshark from the gambling boat was in town yesterday. He's Russian Mafia. They would have the potential organization, resources, and personnel."

I nodded slowly, absorbing that idea. "Unfortunately, they'd also be aware that they will be top of the suspect list. Mr. Morosov was in here yesterday and said they're getting the boat ready to go out this weekend."

"Think they could use three bags of faerock for their Infernal engines?" Gord raised his hands, palm up, daring me to consider the notion. "Those cauldrons have to be huge compared to what's in our cars."

I let that idea roll over in my mind for a few minutes. Morosov was in town right after or maybe even while the faerock train was here. Three bags missing, and the news report said the only two inventory checks were at Windsor and Fort Erie. Both are border towns, and they'd have to record manifests as they crossed the international borders.

It just didn't make sense for the weresharks to go after that when they were likely going to be the primary suspects.

"Don't you see?" Gord came over and sat on the stool opposite me at the front counter. "That wereshark dude stopped in here to give himself an alibi, while his team of snoops and sneaks boarded the train, grabbed three bags, and hightailed it out. What is that guy? Some top enforcer for the mafia?"

I pulled the card out of my purse and looked at his title. "Assistant director of security for *The Tisserand.*"

"Perfect!" Gord slapped the counter. "A security director? He's probably a spy or something. Excels at breaking and entering. He might even have been trying to send one of his spies into your house. To plant some evidence or something."

I shook my head. "Why would he want to plant evidence at my place? And Courtney and Willard really think it was a pixie trying to break into my house last night."

"Pixies can be bought. And they are small enough to hide just about anywhere. You never know, one could be in here right now."

I laughed and pointed at Cleo, stalking slowly, her body low to the floor.

"You really think an undead cat with vampire senses and reflexes wouldn't sense a pixie trying to hide in here?" I shook my head. "How do you think we knew someone was trying to break into my place last night?"

"Oh, yeah..."

The bell on the front door jingled, and my mouth dropped open when I glanced that way.

Lenora Needles peered in, standing outside, holding the

door open. She shut her eyes for a second, took a deep breath, then jerked the door open wider and strode in.

"Samantha... I must apologize for my earlier behaviour."

I raised an eyebrow and glanced at Gord. He wore a puzzled look since I hadn't told him about my encounter with the gossip earlier. I pursed my lips and looked back at Mrs. Needles, not saying anything.

"I'm so sorry. But... I... I need your help." Her eyes stared at the counter or the back of my laptop computer. I wasn't sure what she was looking at.

"Help with what?" I asked tentatively.

"That girlfriend of yours! She's arrested my Robert." Mrs. Needles spat the words out, obviously distressed. "You've solved those two other crimes here. You've got to help Robert. He didn't steal that faerock. Neither of us have any idea how that empty bag got into his car."

18

I steered Mrs. Needles to one of our easy chairs.

"I don't know what to do," she whispered as she sat.

"How about a cup of coffee to help calm down?"

"Tea? I put the kettle on right before that woman!... I mean... your girlfriend and that orc plowed their way into my shop, demanding to know whose car was parked behind the shop."

I glanced at Gord. This late in the day, I didn't bother to have any hot water for tea ready.

"Right. Hot water. Good thing I know my way around a coffee bar." He chuckled at his own jest and headed behind the counter to fill our kettle.

Mrs. Needles sat with her purse on her lap, clutching the leather covered handles in an alternating squeeze. First one hand tightened, then the other. For once, no knitting protruded from her bag.

Cleo padded over and sniffed at Mrs. Needles' ankles. *Did she find my present?*

I tried not to glance down and give the distraught woman any reason to bring up a dead mouse.

Gord came over with a steaming paper cup, with the cardboard sleeve around it, and our little basket of various tea bags.

"Camel.... Chamomile if you would?" Mrs. Needles said with a quiver in her voice but a stern glance for Gord. Her voice firmed enough to demand, "And one packet of sugar."

Gord rolled his lower lip in and plucked out the chamomile tea bag from the selection, unwrapped the tea bag, and dropped it into her cup. After he let the little tag on the string drop over the outside of the cup, he returned to the beverage area and snagged a sugar packet. He returned with a towel draped over his arm and a single sugar packet on a cork lined plastic tray I kept under the coffee area.

His voice dropped into a deep approximation of a bored waiter. "Your sugar, madame." He held the tray out, waiting for her to pluck the paper packet from it.

A stern look from me kept him from making any further snarky comments. He set the little packet and a wooden stir stick next to her cup and retreated to the stool at the counter.

He should have brought her an entire four kilo bag of sugar. And I'm not sure even that could sweeten her sourness.

I should have known Cleo would fill the snarky gap. Fortunately, only I could hear her.

"Tell me what happened." I tried to keep my voice polite and inquisitive.

She eyed the sugar packet, then looked up at me. If she was waiting for service to put the sugar in her cup, she was in the wrong place. Even if she had been nice earlier, my klutz curse kept me from even considering doing her the favour of dumping in the packet. And even I wasn't mean enough to try to tempt the klutz gods and risk spilling hot water all over her.

Mrs. Needles slowly reached out for the packet, her own hand quavering only slightly. After another deep breath to steady her nerves, she ripped it open and dumped it in.

She looked up at me after her first sip. "Seriously. I doubt that your clumsiness is a real curse. You could have prepared this yourself."

It took me five years to track down the exact curse incantation used in that tomb trap. Cleo's voice sounded in my head, dripping with snark. *I don't need that witch to second guess half-a-decade of research and magical testing on you. Tell her she's welcome to visit the tomb where your mother set off the trap. We just won't tell her exactly where the curse trigger is.*

I decided to avoid that line of response and stayed polite and inquisitive.

"What happened with Robert?"

Mrs. Needles closed her eyes, sucked in a deep breath, and let it out slowly. "I suppose I shouldn't say mean things about your girlfriend if I am here requesting your assistance."

"I believe you are walking on very thin ice at the moment," was the politest words I could offer on the spot. "But I'll give you a pass for that one. Please keep on topic and tell me what happened without insulting anyone."

"Well, Constable Montrose," she spat out, then paused, probably waiting to see if I took offence at her using Courtney's formal title. I was actually more miffed at her derogatory tone. But I nodded stiffly so she'd continue.

"The constable and the inspector entered through our back room. Not even the courtesy of coming around to the front like normal folks." She took a sip of tea, tilting the cup above her purse after pushing the handles to bend them out of the way. "They inquired as to whose car was parked behind the store."

"You've got what, about twelve spaces in the lot behind your store?" I asked.

"I asked which car they were inquiring about, since there were at least half a dozen out there." She took another sip of tea. "They described Robert's Toyota, and I feared it had been vandalized. That green inspector asked if Robert could come outside with them. Of course, he did go. Such a nice boy my Robert. He only wanted to help, so he grabbed his keys from the hook by the stairs up to my flat over the store and stepped out with them. The next thing I knew, he was in cuffs, and your girlfriend pulled a bright green bag from the backseat of the Toyota."

"A large faerock bag?"

"It was. Robert explained that he had no idea how that got in his car. But Constable Montrose..." Again with the derogatory tone. She paused, watching me for a reaction. I didn't give her the pleasure of accepting the insult she was trying to build with Courtney's title and surname. "She put the empty faerock bag into one of those big plastic bags with the word *evidence* stamped on it. Like it was official and going to be used against my Robert."

"It probably will be," I said in a dry, matter of fact tone. "What was Robert doing while the Faerock Train was in Eerie Falls?"

"Well, I sent him down to get my faerock order. It's not a large one, but I always ask him to come back to Eerie Falls, so I don't have to worry about letting the infernal out of my sedan."

"I don't believe it's possible to let an infernal escape just by adding faerock fuel to the inlet pipe." I shook my head, trying to picture how that would work. The faerock fuel portal on a fae car looked just like a normal, mundane gasoline intake. In fact, a small tank was attached just in case a mundane tried to fill the tank with gasoline. But push faerock in, and a magical sensor would suck the mineral in and drop it into the magical cauldron where the infernal lived. The Infernal Cauldron Company had all sorts of safeguards and one-way valve spells in place to keep the demons contained and feed it with magical faerock.

"Well, I don't want to risk the potential. My late husband always took care of fuelling up the sedan. He showed Robert how to manage it so I wouldn't have to worry."

"That was probably wise," I said, just to fill the space. If I argued with her, I'd never get her out of the store. "When did Robert get your order?"

"Yesterday of course."

"I meant what time? The train usually departs by one, and he wasn't there when I got our orders."

"Well, it was right after he got up. I had to roust him, because he'd been up late the night before watching the band with his friend from college. The poor fellow that got strangled."

"What time did you roust your son out of bed?" I tried not to give an exasperated sigh when I pushed for clearer answers.

"Right about noon, I think. He was sleeping too long, when I had a list of chores for him to help with. He still needs to clean out the trash bin that we set out at the curb. I like it cleaned at least twice a year."

I was beginning to understand why Robert wanted as much space as possible between himself and his mother.

"So, you woke Robert at noon and got him out to town hall before one when the train left?"

"Of course. It's not that far of a walk. We're only a block away from town hall, and the rails are right next to my shop. We had one of those boxcars with the green bags sitting next to our building the entire time. I'm surprised the train noises didn't wake him. All of that metal clacking and brake squealing. I almost went and got my wand and used it to unlock his bedroom door yesterday. He didn't want to rouse himself with my pounding. He was much easier to awaken today. Got him up bright and early to start on his chores. Of course, I let him venture down to the doughnut shop on his way to do my shopping."

"I see. Staying up late can really make you want to sleep in." Her story wasn't doing much to convince me that Robert didn't have time to pilfer a few bags from the faerock train. But he'd never seemed like the type of guy who'd be into train robbery. I glanced back at Gord. He had his lower lip rolled in and an eyebrow raised. Evidently he was going down the same thought-path I was.

"Well, my Robert is innocent! I told your girlfriend that. I'll have her badge when he's proven to be innocent."

"And you believe a threat like that is going to make me help you?" I stood and held a hand out towards the door. "I believe I've heard enough of your story, Lenora."

She set her cup on the table, then stood. As she moved her purse, she paused, opened it, and peered in. Satisfied with what she saw, her eyes darted around until they landed on Cleo.

Oh, good. She found my present. I'll try to get another when—or if —she comes back again. Maybe I should give her two next time.

"If you can't clear my Robert's name, then I will have her

badge, young lady." Mrs. Needles glared at me. Her gaze almost seemed to be daring me to slap her.

I resisted the urge and put my best *dealing with an annoying customer* smile on my face. "Lenora, I'd help Robert because he's my friend, and that's what friends do for each other. As for you, keep your behind out of my store. Send one of your employees down to get the needlecraft books whenever I message your shop. You are no longer welcome here."

"What? I never! How dare you?!" Her face was glowing red. Her hand darted into her bag.

I had no idea what she was thinking, but it couldn't be pleasant thoughts.

Cleo's thought pounded into my mind. A single magical command that I recognized. It wouldn't work for her since she couldn't speak human words out loud. Did I need to say it?

Lenora's face was deep red, and her hand emerged, gripping her wand tightly.

My lips parted, and I said the arcane command word.

Books flew off the shelf. Not just a few. Almost all the hardcover trade books and about half of the paperbacks. They swirled, stacked, and the eight, no ten-foot tall book golem took a step forward. It towered over us, just behind me. Gord scooted to the side of the store, standing in front of my office door, his face gone white.

Lenora Needles stared up at the book golem and swallowed whatever she was about to say. She took a step back towards the door, then another, and another until she backed into the doorknob.

"You're as bad as your grandmother," Mrs. Needles hissed between clenched teeth.

"Lenora," Gramps said from the bottom of the staircase

up to his study. "Your husband Leonard was one of my dearest friends. Even he would tell you to behave civilly."

"Merlin Cupertino, you heard your granddaughter threaten me. She summoned that thing!" Little drops of saliva flew from her mouth as she ranted. "She aims to do me harm."

"She cannot. That is a guardian. It will only protect the staff and the store. Strike my granddaughter or myself, or use your wand and attempt a hostile spell, and you'll feel its purpose." Gramps stepped out around the golem. "For your own sake, and that of your son, I suggest you leave. Perhaps you should have a nip or two of that vodka you keep under the register in your shop."

"Why? I never drink. How dare you accuse me!"

"Leonard would be disappointed. First you threaten my granddaughter, then you lie about your bottle."

"I have had enough of the Cupertinos! Good day to you both!"

Mrs. Needles pulled the door open and tried to slam it shut, but the piston on it kept it moving slowly. She glared through the window, then stormed off.

Too bad the door didn't hit her in the—

I glared at Cleo, shaking my head. After I let out the breath I was holding, my knees buckled. I collapsed into the cushioned chair behind me.

Cleo's mirth was echoing in her next statement. *You did very well with her. Don't forget to dismiss your golem, dear.*

19

"You won't believe all the stuff I saw and heard at the knitting shop!"

DeAnn slid into the booth, on the opposite side from me, setting her purse on the cushioned bench next to her.

"Bob Needles got arrested. Mrs. Needles cursed my name along with Courtney's and then drank all the vodka she keeps hidden in the cabinet under her computer?"

DeAnn's smile drooped, and she looked at me, mouth open.

All I could do was shrug. "Mrs. Needles came down to my store about half an hour ago, threatening to have Courtney fired from the Provincial Police if I didn't clear her son's name."

"How dare she! Why that woman makes me so mad!" DeAnn's face slid from a look of bewilderment to outright anger. "Courtney is so caring about this town and all the people here. She had no right to call her out for doing her job."

I nodded slowly, not sure what else I could say.

"Well, whatever you told that old busybody set her off. She didn't even try to hide her bottle. Even after the tirades she launched about how she shouldn't even allow covered coffee cups in her shop. One woman, I forget her name, had a stash of fudge in her purse. She offered me a piece, and it was delicious. That old busybody saw us and made us go outside. No food in the shop!"

"That figures," I said with a shake of my head. I didn't want to talk about Mrs. Needles, but I was still wracking my brain, trying to figure out the mystery of the train heist. Bob just didn't fit the picture of a train robber. I smiled, though, thinking about Mrs. Needles needing to finish a bottle of vodka after staring down my shop's book golem. "Figures that Mrs. Needles had a bottle stashed. She's too high-strung to not have some alcohol around."

DeAnn nodded agreement. "After she pulled it out and took a swig straight from the bottle, Marcia, the employee at the store, just rolled her eyes and pushed the old gossip back into the classroom. Whatever you did had her spitting your last name as a cuss word."

Another sigh escaped from me. I hadn't wanted an altercation with Mrs. Needles, but here we were. "I kicked her out of my store, permanently."

"Ooooo! No wonder she was mad. She doesn't seem to be the type to take that well." DeAnn paled and looked at me, her eyes searching. "You're not hurt, are you? Is the store still standing? That woman could do violence. I'm sure she could murder if need be and then blame someone else. She didn't hurt you?"

"I'm fine. So is the store." How could I explain without mentioning the book golem? "Gramps came down and backed me up. And Gord was there. We had more than enough muscle around to make her leave without destroying the store."

DeAnn laughed, then looked worried. "I'm sorry. I don't picture your grandfather as muscle. Nor would Gord fall into that category."

"I see your point. No worries there." I smiled to show I wasn't insulted. In fact, I agreed with her on the physical side. As for magic, well, Gramps and Grams made one heck of a magical team. I'd stack them up against a single Dymestl witch any day. The Dymestls, the royal family of the fae, produced the most powerful witches and wizards by far of all fae. And when Grams was alive, she and Gramps were strong enough together I'd put them at the top of the non-Dymestl witches.

But Gramps was only half that team, and Cleo had some severe limits now. Like being an undead cat with limited spell casting ability. And the fact that Gramps had no idea his late wife's spirit was now inhabiting that furry body.

"Soooo... Why did young Mr. Needles get arrested?" DeAnn raised an eyebrow, but Zoey walked up right then.

"What are you drinking, hun?"

"I definitely need a mango-thingie after my day at the knitting shop!" She looked at the chalk board by the front door that listed the daily specials. "What's the cook got going for dinner?"

Zoey ran down the list, and we each settled on a burger, along with a plate of poutine to share.

"More wine, sweetie?" Zoey pointed her pen at my tumbler.

"I better switch to pop," I said, remembering my earlier hangover.

"Right, mango-thingie and brown bubbles with a couple of moo-plates and poutine." With our local mundane in the pub, Zoey and the other pixie who was waiting tables had to stay in their human forms. No zipping about on pixie wings.

No sooner had Zoey stepped away than Niki Durand walked up, a slushy orange drink in hand with a little umbrella accenting the top. Her oversized designer T3 brand bag hung over her left shoulder.

"Well, look who the cat drug in!" She swayed slightly as she stood at the end of our booth. Neither DeAnn nor I slid over to offer her a seat. Niki just shrugged and giggled, taking another sip of her drink.

"Can we help you, special assistant?" I kept my voice neutral, not wanting to go through another verbal altercation after dealing with Mrs. Needles.

"You had your chance, Cooper." She grinned and shuffled her feet. "I hope you and that constable of yours have a fun time. This little podunk town is too small for my tastes."

DeAnn gave Niki a polite smile. "I'm sure the MP is anxiously awaiting your report on all things podunk. Perhaps you'll get a promotion out of it. What's above special assistant? Super Duper Assistant?"

"You Amerishans!" Niki's speech was slurring as badly as she wobbled. She giggled at her words.

"Maybe you should slow down on the drinks tonight?" I hated to suggest that, but she was wobbly. "Courtney already had to arrest one friend today. I'd hate for you to get a public intoxication charge."

"Bob, you mean? Poor Bob." Niki raised her glass. "To

Bob! And your girlfriend doesn't need to worry about me. I'm out of here tonight. Just waiting for my ride."

She wobbled, unsteady, on her three-inch spike heels and tight skirt. But her euphoria was catchy. Even I was feeling giddy just watching her wave her little umbrella drink around.

Without another word, Niki turned and headed back towards the bar. There were still a few empty seats there. She had difficulty trying to get her butt on a stool, even after a couple of tries. Bubbles and Chief were right next to the stool she selected. A grinning Bubbles watched her for a moment, then must have offered to help. He slid off his stool, grabbed her at the waist, and effortlessly lifted her up. Shifter strength was more than enough to lift the thin woman onto the stool.

Niki beamed and blew him a kiss in thanks, then turned to lean on the bar, sucking on the straw in her glass.

Zoey stepped up with my coke, and DeAnn's mango-thingie in fresh tumblers. Despite the lid on the metal vessel, Darcy at the bar had stuck a little paper umbrella into the slot along with the straw, making the drink festive.

I pointed up towards the bar. "Has Darcy cut her off yet?"

"Oh, yeah!" Zoey nodded. "Don't know where she was day-drinking, but she's flush to the gills. Darcy gave her a half strength first round, and now she's using the special bottles from under the bar we keep for the bad drunks."

"You mean the booze bottles filled with water, right?"

"Some are brown water." Zoey chuckled, then her face dropped. "What have you heard about Bob Needles? Anything?" Her eyes flipped to DeAnn, in an unspoken understanding that we had to be careful in what we said.

Our author friend nodded quickly. "Exactly! Why ever did he get arrested? I wish this town had a newspaper."

"Check the *Fort Erie Times*," Zoey suggested. When

DeAnn pulled out her phone and started tapping on the letters to bring it up, Zoey and I exchanged a quick glance. Of course, I realized *The Times* had a mundane facing website. DeAnn would only see that side while our fae phones would show us the magical version.

"Oooo! A train robbery. A shipment of precious metals stolen as the train moved along the north-western shore of Lake Erie." DeAnn kept scrolling. "The stolen shipment was valued at over a million Canadian. No wonder that old busy-body at the knitting shop was so concerned. That's a tough charge to face. Do you really think he did that?"

I shrugged and looked at Zoey. She paused, then shook her head. "Bob always had a sensible head on him. And he doesn't seem to have a gambling problem. At least he never did when I was in Toronto. He'd stop in at the place I worked about once a week. Dinner and a drink. Tipped well but not too much."

DeAnn stowed her phone back in her purse. "Did he have a girlfriend? Get anyone in trouble where he might suddenly need to worry about child support or such?"

Zoey shrugged. "Not that I know of. He'd occasionally talk about a date, but he never brought anyone around. He had a few friends he'd hang out with. Some guys, some girls. But nothing special ever seemed to develop."

"Well, *The Times* report said he was arrested for evidence found in his car. Mrs. Needles was carrying on and wailing about how he'd never have a bag like that in his car." DeAnn shrugged. "I mean, Courtney and the Inspector fellow wouldn't arrest someone without evidence. I take it whatever that bag was didn't just blow into the fellow's car on a breeze?"

I shrugged and looked at Zoey. She just shook her head.

"I'll leave the pondering to you two. I've got tables to wait on."

As she headed back to the bar, Gord, Suki, and Randy headed up onto the stage. Randy had a large upright bass now.

DeAnn noticed and nodded toward the bassist. "Oh! That thing is huge. I'm glad they've got a big panel van to haul all of their instruments around."

Suki wore a golden-tinged sax, hanging from a strap around her neck. After they ran their sound checks, she let her fingers waltz across her keyboard.

"Tonight we're going to do something a little different and a little special. Take us in, Sticks."

Gord rapped out the slower beat, and they headed into some instrumental jazz. Half the time Suki stayed on keys, but a few times, she stepped out and raised the sax to her lips. On his side of the stage, Randy's long and thick fingers bounced along the bass strings. Gord tapped and rapped his sticks. Sometimes he swished with his metal brushes.

No one in the bar seemed to mind the change of pace.

"Who," DeAnn asked, "do you think could have robbed that train?"

I shrugged but started to wonder out loud. "Well, Gord seems to think it's that Mr. Morosov that comes into the bookstore some. He works on the gambling boat out of Fort Erie, and everyone knows the gambling boats are tied to the Russian mafia."

"There's a gambling boat?"

Drat! I forgot that she wouldn't have heard about that. "Yeah. They fly under the radar politically and don't advertise much. Especially not in the states."

"Well, I'm sure the Russian Mafia would have an interest in precious metals. Wait!" She paused for a few seconds, then pointed at the stage. "Do you think that murdered drummer might have found out about what they were planning? And they put out a hit on him?"

I raised a skeptical eyebrow. "How would he know anything about what the Russian Mafia was planning?"

"Well, that Morosov fellow was in town a couple of days ago. You said he stopped in and bought a big pile of books, including some of mine. Maybe he had loose lips around an underling, and that Geoff fellow overheard them. Geoff seemed like the type that would eavesdrop then try to get a cut, right?"

Suki's lead with the sax shifted back to her on the keys. "There's a theme in jazz, and everyone likes a little sugar. That was the Stanley Turrentine version, so how about a little Lady Billie Holiday too?"

I sat and enjoyed the music, letting my subconscious roll it around. Zoey ran our food out, and we dug into the poutine first.

"Sugar. I'll never cheat on this sweet sugar of mine," Suki sang as their song wound down.

Drake Huppe chose that moment to wander by our table.

"Hey, klutz girl. You seen that political girl? I'm supposed to drive her up to Toronto, so she can catch a train to Ottawa."

I blinked, glanced at Niki, swaying in her seat at the bar. Then I blinked again.

"Hang on, Drake," I said, holding up a finger. I pulled my phone out and texted Courtney.

20

I know who robbed the train! I tapped out quickly.

We've got him in custody was Courtney's reply.

I know. And you've got the wrong person for Geoff's murder too! My fingers flew across the small keyboard. *Can you get to Taps NOW? The perp is about to leave.*

No. And don't you dare accuse anyone!

Never mind. Willard is here.

I stood and slid my phone into my back pocket. "Come this way, Drake." My tummy started doing flip-flops. I was sure I was correct. But was I?

You just stared down Mrs. Needles and banned her from your shop. You can do this. My own mental voice wasn't very reassuring.

"Hey Niki," I said, sliding in next to her and Bubbles. I dropped a hand on his shoulder. If this went bad, I could use shifter backup.

"What are you doing, Sammi?" Willard's voice sounded right behind me.

"Oh good, Courtney texted you. I hoped she would." I flashed him a smile as Niki waved at Darcy, probably to settle her tab. She pulled her wand, which appeared as a credit card thanks to DeAnn's presence, from her front pocket.

Willard used a friendly but stern tone. "Be very careful, Sammi. You don't want someone pressing charges against you."

"I just wondered why Niki here needed a ride up to Toronto tonight? How'd you get to Eerie Falls in the first place?"

"She drove?" Willard said.

"Did she? Where's her car? She was always hitching rides with Lorne or Courtney or you." I looked at Niki. She still had that silly smile plastered on her face. I found myself smiling. Even Bubbles, who was listening, was showing his pearly whites through the dark hair of his bushy beard.

"I have no idea what you're talking about," Niki said and tapped Darcy's tablet with her card and slid it back into her front pocket.

"Did you snap your wing in half? Is that why you can't fly home?" I said, giggling.

"Fly? Are you crazy?" Niki shook her head and hopped off the stool, swaying slightly but with a big silly grin. "Do I look like a pixie?"

Drat! I was hoping to do this without magical terms coming up since we had DeAnn in the house. "No, you don't. How many disguise spells did you have to layer on to squelch your hair highlights?"

She laughed, and let it devolve into giggles. "I'm not a pixie. I'm a Zeta Iota Gamma. They don't let pixies in!" Her giggles didn't stop, but she kept the volume down.

"So you were disguising back then too." I shook my head,

fighting my own urge to laugh and looked at Willard. Even he wore a silly grin. "How many of your ghostly bits did Niki replace at town hall?"

"What? She didn't need to bring any in." Willard, still grinning, waved off the implication that she should have.

"But she was buying the large boxes of doughnut holes. And using a lot of sugar in her coffee and getting sweet drinks from the bar. She must have finished the one she bought this morning before she made it to Mrs. Needles' shop."

"Liking sugar isn't a crime." Niki kept giggling. She looped an arm through Drake's. His face lit up like it always did when he was getting attention from a girl. Even he laughed for a long minute.

I pressed my lips together, trying to hold back my mirth. "Did you break your wing trying to sneak into my house? Why would you want to get into my place? To plant a faerock bag?"

"Bah! You and that constable of yours, thinking you're as good as I am." She swayed and grinned up at Drake. "You're driving me up to Toronto? I can make it worth your while." The giggle she let out made her seem like a smitten schoolgirl.

Drake's chuckle went on a few seconds longer than he normally would have, and his grin grew after her implied suggestion. "I'm ready, sweetheart! Just need to drop the last bag of faerock dust in the tank, and we'll take off."

"Here," her hand darted into her purse, and she pulled out a glowing faerock, laughing. "Use one of mine!"

I exchanged glances with Willard. He still had a silly grin plastered on his face, but his brow crinkled with worry.

"Laughter is an effect of overexposure to faerock magic," I said, trying to suppress a giggle. "Everyone around you is grinning silly smiles." The giggles came out again. Willard, Bubbles, Huppe, and even Chief laughed with me.

"You're making the sour old Royal Canadian Navy guy laugh!" I said between giggles.

Willard was fighting hard but couldn't hold in his chuckles. "What... is... in....your...purse?"

Behind us, Bubbles and Chief clutched their bellies, laughing uncontrollably.

"No..." Niki's giggles turned into high pitched cackling. "Nothing..." she panted, trying to stop laughing.

"I'll need to see inside your bag..." Willard got that much out before he doubled over, clutching his gut, laughing.

Worry flooded Niki's face.

"NO! Get back! All of you!" She clutched the bag to her chest and twisted her face to hold in her laughter. "If anyone comes close to me, I'll pop small!" She jerked her purse open and revealed mounds of glowing green faerock. Possibly enough to power the city of Toronto for a year or longer. But the faerock looked weird. The nuggets were small kibbles. Like cat food sized little kibbles of faerock. They should be the size of my thumb.

"I've already shrunk them once," Niki said with only a small giggle. "I'm going to walk out of here with this creep, and he's driving me away."

"Creep!" Drake laughed, a silly grin going on his face. "She called me a creep!"

"You are, someone yelled from the back of the pub." Everyone broke out in laughter. Waves and waves of laughter.

Niki took a step toward the door; her giggles were almost mad scientist maniacal. "IF anyone tries to stop me, I'll pop small, and BOOM! This faerock will explode. It can't shrink any more."

The laughter in the pub only increased. I was right. She was a pixie. But we couldn't stop her without fear of having her decimate the entire town. That much faerock packed a lot of energy. We might actually start a nuclear war with the cloud of destruction she'd cause. And I couldn't stop laughing from the faerock exposure. That bag must have been leaking its energy since before DeAnn and I had arrived. Why else would the crowd in here be laughing in the face of annihilation?

Pixie wings flared by me, and Zoey hovered right in front of Niki's nose.

"Hey Niki, I got a message for you!" She swung her tiny fist at Niki, but popped tall at the last instant and planted her fist into Niki's cheek. Sparkles of faerock flew into the air as Niki fell back, stunned.

Zoey, in her tall form, held the bag open, moving it fast to catch the errant pieces of faerock. Once the faerock kibbles were safe, Zoey prodded an unconscious Niki with her foot.

"That's for calling me Joey!" Zoey even said it without giggling.

A few seconds later, still laughing because of the faerock exposure, I had my phone out, snapped a photo of the open bag and gleaming green rocks.

I hit Courtney's name and the send icon. Then added, *At Taps, send everything we need to contain this!*

It took a few seconds.

Roger. Containment team on the way.

Are you okay?

I'm fine. But DeAnn is here.

Around the room, teleport sparkles formed and gnomes of various shapes and girth appeared, including one right next to DeAnn's position. Even she had been laughing. Her eyes wide, she reached out and gingerly poked the gnome with her fore-finger, a look of shock on her face.

Inspector Robert and Courtney appeared next. Robert looked around, then made a beeline towards DeAnn. Good. He'd handle her mundane mind and leave her with magically clouded memories.

Courtney found me grinning. The faerock residual magic was just beginning to affect her. She grabbed me in a big hug, a huge smile on her face. Behind her, two of the gnomes took possession of Niki's purse and wrapped it in one of their green faerock protective bags.

"Containment truck is on the way," one of them said to Courtney.

I felt the urge to giggle lessen but only slightly.

"Why," I said, pointing at the Gnome crew, "aren't the gnomes affected by the faerock? You should be happy and laughing like the rest of us."

"I am happy," the dour faced gnome said, who I realized was the one weighing out our orders at the train. "I'm very happy you recovered the missing shipment. It was her, correct, Constable?"

Courtney nodded and giggled some more. "Yep. I'd be mad at her, but I can't right now."

21

The next afternoon, Courtney and I sat at a table in Brigitte's BBQ restaurant. We'd already finished when Gord showed up and set his tray on the two-seater next to ours.

"So, sleepy head..." I grinned at him, happy that the giggles had finally diminished with a night's sleep. "How did you do with the band last night?"

"Great once Courtney got Marius released." He chuckled and pointed with his knife over towards Taps. "Good thing Darcy knew what he'd need. I had no idea the synthetic they serve at jail is so bad."

"Technically, it has everything a vampire needs to stay healthy," Courtney said.

"Have you ever tried it?" Gord looked at her, one eyebrow raised.

"Yuck! No."

"Well, Marius said it was the most awful drink he's ever had. Even worse than sucking rat blood."

I poked his ankle with my foot. "Ewwwww! Gross, mister drummer. Some things don't need to be shared."

Gord looked at Court. "So, we only got about half the story of last night. How did Niki kill off Geoff?"

Courtney shrugged and pointed at me. "Better ask Sherlock Cupertino here."

"It's complicated, but bear with me."

"Don't I always?" Gord said, his bite of brisket hovering in front of his mouth.

"You do. And I'm glad." I gave him a smile, then continued so he could eat and listen. "Back in college, Niki convinced Geoff to embezzle funds from the student government, and they covered it up pretty well, blaming Zoey. That was when Bob Needles intervened. So when Niki found Geoff again in Toronto, she hatched a plan to heist the faerock from the train."

"How did you even figure that out?" Courtney asked, then took another bite of her sandwich.

I shrugged. "Courtney said that Geoff and Niki were on finance committees together. Once I figured out Niki was behind the faerock robbery, it was easy to figure out who was pushing him to mess with the books. You should ask Bob Needles what he remembers about his audit. You might be able to get the evidence to pin that on her, too."

Courtney nodded, and pulled her phone out. Probably going to send a message to the Inspector about what I'd just suggested.

"Yeah, but why Geoff?" Gord shook his head. "He was such a creep."

"Because he was heir to one of the families involved in creating the containment spells on the Infernal brand cauldrons. He knew the trade secrets that Niki needed to shrink the faerock down and smuggle it off the train." I looked at Courtney for confirmation.

"Only because the report has been filed and released, can I talk about it," she said, giving me a firm look. "The gnomes found a cracked board on the side of one of the boxcars. That happened to be the one the faerock was missing from. Niki is not talking, but we were able to piece together how it happened after conversing with magical techs at the Infernal company."

She took another sip of her pop, then continued. "Niki snuck in through the crack in the board. Boy! I had no idea at all she was a pixie. Such a poser. She didn't want to hang out with the pixies at their sorority. So she masqueraded as a human-sized fae and got in with the ZIG girls."

"Probably good that you didn't pledge along with her," I suggested.

Courtney shrugged. "I kinda wanted to but knew I'd be too devoted to classwork to mess with Greek life. I realize that I missed out on some great opportunities for lifelong friendships, though."

Gord waved his fork in the air. "Back to the train. How'd she get the faerock?"

"She got into the train and popped tall so she could dump a bag of faerock into her purse." Courtney pulled her phone out and scrolled through a screen or two. Probably looking at the police report, since her screen looked boring and official. "Here it is. The gnome faerock chief said that while the faerock is in their bags, it's protected from outside magic. It has a tendency to magnify any spell effects in its proximity, so the bags are specifically warded. Geoff probably knew that and passed it on while Niki was learning from him."

"So, what happened? Niki decided she didn't need Geoff any longer?"

"Exactly my thought," I said and looked at Courtney. "Did you find any pixie fingerprints on that guitar pick in Geoff's hands?"

She tapped her phone and scrolled. "Smudges the size of pixie fingerprints, but no prints on the pick besides Geoff's own. We think Niki sent him a magical message late, suggesting a tryst out in their van, then surprised him in pixie form. She probably whipped the guitar string around his neck, popped tall for leverage and killed him."

I nodded and pointed over at Taps. "Suki did something like that flick and spin with her cable for the keyboards. She was skilled in flicking it around the leg to the stand and catching it."

Courtney nodded. "Even though she's not talking, the report says that the lack of prints other than the victim's shows the pick was cleaned, then placed in his hand post-mortem."

Gord nodded. "Fly up with it while she's in pixie form, shove it in his hand, but her prints are too small to read. Then pop tall and push his hand closed?"

I gave him a smile. "Niki probably realized she needed to distract her old roomie, not expecting to find Courtney in the town where she was about to pull off a million-dollar heist. So framing Marius would give Courtney a lead to pursue and leave the cop that knew her, chasing a murder rather than paying attention to the faerock train."

Gord looked back at me. "How did you figure out it was Niki?"

"Sugar, just like the song Suki sang." I grinned, glad that the urge to laugh had diminished after the faerock was secured. "She only drank sweet drinks, four packs of sugar in a coffee, no less. And she was always getting doughnut holes."

"And the faerock giggles," Courtney added. "She had so much residual faerock exposure she was drunk on it, not on booze. Anywhere but a bar, that might have been more evident."

"Well," I poked his ankle with my foot. "What about you and the band?"

"I need to talk to mom, but they invited me to stick with them this summer while they're in Eerie Falls."

"Their other drummer not coming back?" Courtney asked, looking confused.

"Not yet. Getting trampled by an elephant can screw a guy up." Gord shrugged but had a wistful smile growing. "If we can get one of the pixies to come in for my shift each Thursday to Sunday, I can gig with the band at Darcy's. I'll get the drummer's cut of the fees the band gets, so Mom will have the budget to bring in a pixie or two. At least until their old drummer is well enough to play again."

"Did you check on that?" I asked Courtney. She nodded.

Courtney glanced at me. "You mean the golfer who targeted the elephant? He has had his legal fees and penalties paid by an anonymous donor, and it looks to be linked to campaign funds from the PAC that supports Niki's former MP."

"I suspected something like that," I said with a grin. "You think Niki might have made political arrangements to get the PAC to cover the golfer's legal woes? I wonder why she'd do that?"

Gord snorted. "Obviously because she was the one who set the golfer up to enrage the elephant. She needed a gig for Geoff and had heard that Suki and the band were coming down here. Where the faerock train was going to be."

He glanced at me, dropping both eyebrows. "So, why'd Niki try to break into your place?"

Courtney and I shared a glance and a smile. I pointed at my girlfriend, then wrapped my fingers around hers. "To frame me and get even with Courtney for some imagined slight in the past."

"Or just distraction. She knew I'd go nuts if my girlfriend was implicated in the robbery. And I'd be on the suspect list too." Courtney chuckled. "Fortunately, I've been reinforcing the warding spells on Sammi's windows and doors. I've got access to top spells to install on my residence, so I used them."

"But that's not your residence," I said, raising an eyebrow.

"Yet," Gord said with a laugh.

"You were going to invite me to move in, weren't you?" Courtney watched my face, her own sliding back into her unreadable cop expression.

I let a smile grow on mine. "Of course, I was waiting for your lease to get close to expiring."

"My opt-out option goes live in two weeks." She tilted her head, waiting.

"So... um.... You wanna move into my place? Share the expenses?"

"I thought you'd never ask!"

THE END
Sammi and Courtney's adventures will continue soon!

*I*F *YOU ENJOYED THIS STORY, FLIP THE PAGE TO CHECK OUT A sample of the first book in my* Mystic Brews *series,* Lattes and Spirits.

April Storm just wanted to open a quiet little coffee bar in rural Wales with her batty Aunt Rose. But life in Misty Valley throws a huge twist at the American barista when a ghost asks April to help solve their murders. Add in a snarky talking cat, pixies, magical secret agents, and April's new life anything but quiet!

LATTES AND SPIRITS

The alarm clock blared. I popped open one eye.

4:30. I slapped the snooze. Then slapped it again because I had only drifted off about two hours ago. I hated jet lag.

"Ebrel, cariad!" Aunt Rose's voice kept me from pulling the pillow around my head and drifting back to sleep. *Cariad*, the Welsh form of "love", used like an American auntie would use *dearie*. Her accent and use of my British name pinged my brain enough to make me move. Guilt is a wonderful motivator. I couldn't let her down.

"I'm up!" I shouted and reached for the bedside light. Where was the switch? Probably one of those old-lady-on-the-cord ones. I'd never find it in the dark. Four hours ago, I had used the wall switch for the overhead.

I didn't think I could make it to the wall switch without great risk of breaking one or more of my toes by slamming them into one of the multitude of antique furniture and whatnots that Aunt Rose had crammed into this room.

Instead, I let my magic tingle through my fingers. I found the bulb inside the shade. The little magical ball of light I made could stay in there, hidden from sight. The lamp shade glowed. As long as Aunt Rose didn't turn it off, she wouldn't know I'd used magic. That was something I needed to keep secret.

Now that I could see, I grumbled and reached for my toiletries bag.

"I left a towel out for you, cariad," Rose called again. "Come on down when you can. I be dying to learn this new foo-foo drink machine."

Ugh! First morning in the café. I was the only one who knew how to run the espresso machine, but with jet lag and only two hours of sleep. Back in the States, I'd be heading to bed about now.

"Put on your big-girl-barista pants, April," I muttered and stumbled my way to the bath. Rose's flat above the café had the toilet in another room next to the bath. That was the "loo," she explained. The bath was where one bathed or washed up. Quaint. Living in Wales would take some getting used to.

The warmth of the shower felt so good I didn't want to leave it. Another week, and I might be over my jet lag. Until then, all I could do was work through it. I was committed. Misty Valley was my new home.

A moment later, dry and with the towel wrapped around me, I opened the door. Jake stood in the hallway. I sucked in a breath and tried to hold in my squeal of shock. No need to alarm Aunt Rose. It wasn't every girl who was haunted by the ghost of her dead boyfriend.

"Don't drop chicken feathers in my aunt's hallway," I whispered and slid into my room. I shut the door quickly and spun around. Jake floated there, still covered in chicken feathers. Even his leather jacket, the one he wore when his bike swerved off the road, was coated in ghostly feathers.

"Happy Birthday, April," he said.

"Well, you're not about to see me in my birthday suit. I need to get dressed."

"I've seen it before," he said. "What's the big deal?"

"One, we're not dating anymore," I said. "Two, you're dead, and it's creepy."

"What's the problem?" Jake was so dense sometimes. "I just came to—"

A spark of magic leapt from my finger to the zipper on his jacket, and he winked out of sight.

"You too," I said and touched the ghostly chicken that materialised with him.

That would only give me a minute before he returned. Pesky ghost. And most girls thought living boyfriends could be annoying.

I had my yoga pants on and wiggled my arms and head through my long cable-knit sweater when I smelled wet feathers again.

"What did you do that for?"

"You wouldn't understand," I said when I popped my head through the sweater.

"I just wanted to hang out with you on your birthday," he said. This time two chickens popped in with him. One was pecking at dust under the bedside table. The other was perched on the curved wood of the headboard.

"I know, it's your death day too, and you don't want to be alone."

"The chickens aren't much company," he said and sat next to me on the bed.

"I wish you were useful while you're here. Pardon," I said and reached through his misty green form for my boots. "Look, I can't be shooing you away every few minutes. Today is very important. Don't screw it up for me."

"How would I do that?"

"First, don't ask me questions." I stood and poked a finger at his face. Jake flinched, probably afraid I'd spark him again. "The talking-to-myself excuse only works once a day."

The chicken on the headboard flapped and jumped onto Jake's shoulder.

"And take that feather," I said, pointing to my pillow.

"Sorry," he said. When his fingers touched the feather, it went ghostly again.

"Did you ever figure out why only a few ghost feathers turn solid again?"

He stuck it to the others on his leather jacket. "None of the other ghosts know. They guess that it's because I want to be with you. Some of that energy makes something small, like a feather, become real again. At least I can zap 'em back to the ghost realm when they do pop over."

"Keep an eye out for feathers," I said. "Aunt Rose will have a hissy fit if she thinks I brought a chicken in here."

"As allergic as you are to cats, I doubt she'd blame you for chickens."

"Yesterday was the first time I met her since I was five. She normally only called me on my birthday."

"Ebrel, cariad!" Rose's voice called from the café. "Are you coming down?"

"Don't get me in trouble!" I whispered in a hiss and poked Jake again.

Downstairs, Aunt Rose and our employee, Nia, waited behind the counter.

ALYN TROY

"The drink you made yesterday was magical," Nia said in her high voice. "Will you make me another?"

"Not yet." I waved them out of my way and grabbed my teal apron. Aunt Rose used the teal along with a pink in her decor and signage for Mystic Brews, the new name of her café. New, because I was here to be her partner and chief barista.

"Nia, be a dear and go check on the pastries I put in the oven," Aunt Rose said. Nia bobbed her head of dark wavy hair. She was way too full of bouncing energy for this early in the morning.

My aunt was everything I expected of an "Aunt Rose." A tad on the plump side. Ageing beauty lined her face, crinkled with laugh and smile lines. Her blue eyes matched mine, and a few strands of auburn streaked her grey hair. She would have cut a fine figure, as my father said, in her younger days. Now, she had that grandmotherly air about her, despite not having any children of her own.

Behind her apron, she wore a long-sleeved cardigan over a white blouse. The sweater had roses knitted on the collar and cuffs. She passed me a plate. "Have a scone, cariad. Once we get going, we won't be stopping. The whole village wants to meet you. I've got cream in the back if you want to spice it up."

"This is fine," I said, then turned and did a quick inventory. I nibbled on the scone while prepping. Pitchers, spoons in the ice bath, thermometers, porta-filters, the handled metal bowls where I packed the espresso grounds before the machine worked its high-pressured magic on them—all of it was there. And the pastry was divine. I remembered Mom saying her aunt's baking was the best ever. Anywhere. Full stop. She was correct. This was the best I ever tasted.

Aunt Rose answered a knock on the door.

"Red! Meet my niece Ebrel."

"Pleased ta meet the famed Ebrel, lassie," the man said. He held out a thick hand covered in curly red hair. He had a firm grip and calloused fingers.

"Red is Misty Valley's handyman, cariad," Aunt Rose said. "He's come to look at the ovens for me. We've got a hot spot I need to even out."

"Probably just be a faulty temperature probe," he said.

I washed my hands once he was back in the kitchen. Fortunately, there was a full, though small, pump jar of soap by the sink. I'd never been nailed with a health citation in my years as a barista, and I would not get one here. I glanced at the second grinder by the espresso machine. Then I checked the stock cupboard next to the sink. Regular beans, but no decaf espresso. "I forgot to grab the decaf beans. We do have them, right?"

"I think so. They should be in the cellar," Aunt Rose said. "I can send Nia."

"No worries, I can go check."

Down the stairs, the lights started to glow as I opened the door to the cellar. There was no light switch, and I didn't see magnetic sensors on the door frame. I'd have to check with Red and see how the place was wired. That was a good motion sensor if it caught me at the top of the stairs.

Even though the building was old, the damp, dusky odour I expected was absent. Instead, the aroma of coffee, flour, and all manner of food stuff wafted to me.

The coffee beans sat right where I had seen them yesterday. One row of bags extended out a few inches. I pushed them back, and the bags shook and hissed. I leapt back, magic surging into my hands.

A brownish streak darted sideways from the shelf. A cat.

Huh. Aunt Rose said she didn't have any cats. Why was that one here? How did it get in?

I tried to hold my breath and not get any of the dander in my nose as I grabbed a bag of decaf beans, already roasted, and dashed up the stairs.

"There was a cat!" I set the beans on the counter next to Aunt Rose.

"A tabby, brownish?"

I nodded, taking a few deep breaths.

"I'm sorry, cariad." She pulled a tissue from inside her left sleeve. I waved it off. So far, I was doing fine. Why did grand-motherly types always have tissues and whatnots up their sleeves?

"Thank you... Diolch," I said, remembering the Welsh word for thank you. "No need. I escaped without harm." No symptoms of being around a cat at all.

"Oh, that's good for you, cariad." She turned towards the kitchen. "Nia, Punkin got in again. Would you shoo him out? Ebrel is deathly allergic."

"We all be allergic to that furball," Red's voice drifted out. "You'll have a crowd in a jiffy ready to try Miss Ebrel's fancy new coffee. I'll see if I kin chase him off for a wee bit."

I glanced at the clock. Aunt Rose said we opened at six. Fifteen minutes from now. I pushed the buttons on the grinders, filled the filter baskets for the coffee makers. Dark in one, medium roast in the next, and decaf in the third. The aroma of coffee gave my soul a lift.

"Just like back in the States, isn't it?" Jake asked. He was leaning on the counter, looking at my espresso setup. I raised a finger to my lips to shush him.

Aunt Rose stood by the door, her hand on the key to

unlock it, and looked back over her shoulder. Outside, several figures waited, silhouetted against the dim streetlight.

"Ready to start our new partnership, cariad?"

"Let them in. It's time to brew!"

THANKS FOR READING CHAPTER ONE OF LATTES AND SPIRITS. This is book one of the Mystic Brews cozy mystery series, set in the same magical world as Sammi Cuptertino's Eerie Falls Mysteries.

You can download the book for free from most retailers.

ALSO BY ALYN TROY

Visit AlynTroy.com for each series:

Mystic Brews

Pixie Twist

Eerie Falls

Please visit AlynTroy.com to sign up for my newsletter and keep up to date on news from Misty Valley

MORE FROM ALYN TROY

If you haven't already, you can sign up for my email newsletters. Emails are delivered by interwebz pixies about three times a month. More often around book launches.

If you enjoyed this story, would you please leave a review? For authors, reviews are what Caramel Tornados are to pixies. They not only keep us writing, but they also help us land promotional deals and attract the attention of media.

- Alyn Troy

Milton Keynes UK
Ingram Content Group UK Ltd.
UKHW020840240823
427351UK00015B/675

9 798223 407904